PENGUIN BOOKS
HUMANS AND OTHER ANIMALS

Chi P. Pham is a Tenured Researcher at the Institute of Literature, Vietnam Academy of Social Sciences, Hanoi. She received her first Ph.D. degree in Literary Theory in Vietnam and her second Ph.D. degree in Comparative Literature in University of California, Riverside (USA). She is the secretary of the Association for the Study of Literature and Ecology in ASEAN (ASLE-ASEAN). Her publications include, *Aesthetic Experience in Ramayana Epic* (Hanoi National University Press, 2015); *Literature and Nation-building in Vietnam: The Invisibilization of the Indians* (Routledge, 2021). She is also the co-editor of *Reading South Vietnam's Writers: The Reception of Western Thought in Journalism and Literature* (Springer Nature, 2023). She has edited four collections of Indian and South East Asian folktales in Vietnamese translation, and has co-edited a collection of Vietnamese environmental short stories in English translation entitled *Revenge of Gaia: Contemporary Vietnamese Ecofiction* with Chitra Sankaran (Penguin Random House, 2021). She has also co-edited *Ecologies in Southeast Asian Literatures: Histories, Myths and Societies* with Chitra Sankaran and Gurpreet Kaur (Vernon Press, 2019) and *The Vietnamese Literature: Readings from the Inside* (special issue in *SUVANNABHUMI Multi-disciplinary Journal of Southeast Asian Studies* 14.1, 2022) with Uma Jayaraman. Her latest publications in the field of Environmental Humanities include 'Political Orientation in Ecocriticism: National Allegory in Vietnamese Ecofiction by Trần Duy Phiên.' *CLCWeb: Comparative Literature and Culture* 24.5 (2022) and *Environment and Narrative in Vietnam* (co-edited with Ursula K. Heise, co-author of one chapter, and single author of another chapter) contracted for publication by Palgrave Macmillan

Chitra Sankaran (PhD London), has served as (acting) Head of Department and as Chair of Literature, Department of *English, Linguistics and Theatre Studies*, National University of Singapore. She is the Founding and Current President of the *Association for the Study of Literature and Ecology in ASEAN* (ASLE-ASEAN) and the Chief Editor of the *Journal of Southeast Asian Ecocriticism* (JSEAE). Her publications include three monographs, ten edited volumes, chapters-in-books and research articles in International Journals such as *Interdisciplinary Studies in Literature and Environment*, (ISLE),

Journal of Commonwealth Literature, ARIEL, Theatre Research International. Her recent publications include a monograph on *Women, Subalterns and Ecologies in South and Southeast Asian Women's Fiction* (University of Georgia Press, USA) and a co-authored volume, *Revenge of Gaia: Contemporary Ecofictions from Vietnam* (Penguin Random House).

ALSO by Chi P. Pham and Chitra Sankaran

Revenge of Gaia: Contemporary Vietnamese Ecofiction

Humans And Other Animals: Animal Fiction From Vietnam

Chi P. Pham, Chitra Sankaran

PENGUIN CLASSICS

USA | Canada | UK | Ireland | Australia
New Zealand | India | South Africa | China | Southeast Asia

Penguin Classics is part of the Penguin Random House group of companies
whose addresses can be found at global.penguinrandomhouse.com

Published by Penguin Random House SEA Pte Ltd
9, Changi South Street 3, Level 08-01,
Singapore 486361

First published in Penguin Classics by Penguin Random House SEA 2024

Copyright © Chi P. Pham, Chitra Sankaran 2024

ISBN 9789815144918

Typeset in Minion Pro by MAP Systems, Bengaluru, India

www.penguin.sg

Contents

Humans and Other Animals: A Critical Introduction

Animal Studies and Ecocriticism

Animal Studies—an important interdisciplinary field that has gained prominence in recent decades—is dedicated to the study of animals from diverse disciplinary focal points. The broad objectives of the field are to examine human-animal relationships both historically and in contemporary times across different cultures and traditions. It explores the idea of 'animality' and 'animalization' in order to grapple with the often, rather liminal boundary that divides humans from animals. Animal Studies engages with cultural representations of the animals and by doing so, it seeks to understand not only the broad unspecific category of the 'animal' but also the very limited and specific category of the 'human'.

Most Western and indeed many Eastern traditions have constructed the 'animal' largely as Other to the human. In the value-dualisms that mark the civilized from the savage, order from disorder, civic society from wilderness, the human is placed squarely on the side of the positive binary whilst the animal is exiled to the outer boundaries of civilization, to savagery and violence. The animal in its most feared aspect is constructed as the 'beast' that needs to be hunted and killed in order to safeguard civilization.

Jacques Derrida (2002), the French philosopher, in his final lecture series, *The Animal That Therefore I Am*, examines how human interactions with animal life define humanity and the concept of the human self. Derrida also raises awareness about human treatment of animals in modern industrialized societies raising doubts about what indeed are the limits of humanity, thereby challenging the entrenched view of human superiority.[1]

Such questions regarding the ethics of animal treatment were addressed very early in the 1970s by the Australian philosopher, Peter Singer (1975), a pioneer in the field of Animal Studies. In his book, *Animal Liberation: A New Ethics for Our Treatment of Animals*, Singer argues for the humane treatment of animals because they have the ability to experience suffering. In this, he was following the thought process first generated by the philosopher, Jeremy Bentham. Singer brings to our notice the term 'speciesism' and urges us to treat it on par with other such terms that describe unfair discrimination, such as racism and sexism. He reasserts the fact that humans as a whole only selfishly care for the welfare of their own species

---

[1]   Jacques Derrida and David Wills. 'The Animal That Therefore I Am (More to Follow)', *Critical Inquiry*, Vol. 28, No. 2, Winter, 2002, pp. 369–418.

to the detriment of all others over which they claimed stewardship.[2] Peter Singer denounces anthropocentrism: '[T]he pattern of prejudice in humans' treatment of animals is identical to that of racism and sexism', he declares.[3]

Scholars in the field of Animal Studies make a point about the differential treatment accorded to different categories of animals. Thus, while for the most part, 'pets' are cosseted and pampered, and cared for like human children, 'game animals' are killed for pleasure on safari hunts. Likewise, the cruelty inflicted on laboratory animals is routinely excused as necessary for the pursuit of higher Science. One of the worst fates met by farm animals is indeed through factory farming. Thus, Animal Studies scholars are careful to highlight the differences in the treatment meted out to different categories within this broad group labeled 'animal'.

One of the great dangers widely identified by scholars is the anthropocentric approach to animals. In Donna Haraway's famous words, 'We polish an animal mirror to look for ourselves.'[4] Haraway's words unflinchingly hold the mirror up to humanity's deeply entrenched anthropocentric tendency. Anthropocentrism is widely understood as the ethical belief that only humans possess intrinsic value. From this perspective, nonhuman animals have only economic and/or symbolic value. They are not

---

[2] Peter Singer. *Animal Liberation: A New Ethics for Our Treatment of Animals*. New York: Harper Collins, 1975.

[3] Ibid, 6.

[4] Donna Haraway. *Simians, Cyborgs, and Women: The Reinvention of Nature*. New York: Routledge, 1991, 21.

cognized as autonomous agents in their own right. Boria Sax has described anthropocentrism as the 'tendency to vastly exaggerate human dominance, understanding, power, autonomy, unity, guilt, virtue, wickedness, and morality'[5]. Factory farming, the use of animals for laboratory experiments, and other cruelties meted out to animals, have now become ubiquitous the world over. Nevertheless, in many Asian countries, paradoxically, a parallel elevation of the animal to autonomy and agentic status continues in certain cultural spaces, albeit inconsistently. We will explore this aspect more closely in the sections below, specifically with regard to Vietnamese culture.

Animals in Vietnamese Culture

Vietnamese culture is heterogeneous, made up of disparate groups with multiple ethnicities. Although most Vietnamese subcultures consider animals, whether domestic or wild, and notwithstanding their habitats, as a source of food, of utility, and even cash income,[6] animals are also simultaneously esteemed in the symbolic realm and this symbolism often has a political function. For example, the largest Vietnamese ethnic group considers lions and tortoises (*ly, quy*) as among the noblest and the most sacred along with the dragon (*long*) and the phoenix (*phụng*). Of the latter two, which belong to the realm of

---

[5] Boria Sax. 'What is this quintessence of dust? The concept of the "human" and its origins.' In Rob Boddice (Ed.) *Anthropocentrism: Human, Animals, Environments*. Leiden, Boston: Brill, 2011, pp. 36.

[6] American Institutes for Research Headquarters. *Minority Groups in North Vietnam*, Department of the Army, 1972, pp. 271–277

imaginary animals, the dragon is hailed as the ancestor of the Vietnamese people. Indeed, feudal emperors are often celebrated as children of dragons. Hence, their iconic images depict them wearing costumes designed with dragon patterns. In royal historical records, Vietnamese kings are usually equated with a dragon. For example, in *Việt điện u linh tập* (Story Collection of the Magic Viet Country) published in 1329, the term 'hidden dragon' is used to refer to Lý Thái Tổ (974–1028) before he became king.[7] Again, in *Việt Nam khai quốc chí truyện* (Recorded Tales of the Founding of the Nation), written in the eighteenth century, a folk poem uses dragon imagery to describe the minister Nguyễn Hoàng's revolutionary spirit who overthrew the corrupt, contemporary king of his times: 'How could the heavenly dragon be content to lie low in a pond?/ Just hearing the wind or thunder would have him soar skyward'[8]. According to the linguist, Nguyễn Văn Trào (2014), most idioms related to dragons in Vietnam highlight this animal as symbolizing an upper-class status and good fortune. Some of the idioms that indicate this include 'the dragon visits the shrimp's house' *(rồng đến nhà tôm),* which means that high-ranking people in a hierarchical society visit those who are inferior to them; and 'the tomb buried at the

---

[7] Ostrowski and Zottoli, 'Story Collection of Magic Viet Country', in *Sources of Vietnamese Tradition.* George Edson Dutton, Jayne Susan Werner, John K. Whitmore. Columbia University Press, 2012, pp. 63.

[8] Catherine Churchman. 'Recorded Tales of the Founding of the Country,' in *Sources of Vietnamese Tradition.* George Edson Dutton, Jayne Susan Werner, John K. Whitmore. Columbia University Press, 2012, pp. 158.

dragon jaw' *(mả táng hàm rồng)*, would refer to those who always have good luck.[9]

Fantastic beasts like the dragon, that are held in high esteem and sacralized, are seen as exclusive to the dominant cultural group (*Kinh*) in Vietnam. Opposed to this exclusivity, stands the buffalo that appears to have been loved and culturally centered by most other ethnic groups (like *Tày, Mường, Nùng, Ede* and *Bahna*), given their association with the traditional rice-growing economy. Here, we descend from the symbolic realm to the real, also demonstrating power gradations in society that are played out through animals. In most Vietnamese cultures, water-buffaloes form the main labour force working the rice paddle and hauling the paddy.[10] Thus, traditionally, the buffalo is respected. Historical records show that many Vietnamese royal courts, by law, recognized the need to provide security for these beasts of burden and issued edicts punishing any cruelty against livestock.[11] In textbooks, children learn folk songs praising the buffalo not only as an important labour-provider but in fact, as a valued member of farming families. The lyrics of these folk songs insist on human-animal reciprocity:

> 'O You buffalo! I ask of you
> to please go out to the field
> Plowing with me

---

[9] Nguyễn Văn Trào. 'Nghĩa biểu trưng văn hóa của các từ chỉ động vật trong tiếng Anh và tiếng Việt.' Tạp chí *Khoa học xã hội Việt Nam*, số 4(77), 2014, pp. 93–103.

[10] American Institutes for Research Headquarters. Ibid.

[11] Ngô Sĩ Liên, *Đại Việt Sử kí toàn thư*. Jone K. Whitmore. 41

Plowing for crops as an essential work of agricultural capital
I labour this side and you labour that side, equally, so we do not care who contributes more
When will the rice plant bloom? You can eat the remaining grass in the field.'

(Trâu ơi! Ta bảo trâu này!
Trâu ra ngoài ruộng trâu cày với ta
Cấy cày vốn nghiệp nông gia
Ta đây trâu đấy ai mà quản công!
Bao giờ cây lúa trổ bông
Thời còn ngọn cỏ ngoài đồng trâu ăn)

or

'O buffalo! I beseech you
Eat until you are full, then you plow deeply
To live this life, cleverness is not needed
What makes you prosper is diligence and hard work.'

(Trâu ơi! Ta bảo trâu này
Trâu ăn cho béo trâu cày cho sâu
Ở đời khôn khéo chi đâu
Chẳng qua cũng chỉ hơn nhau chữ cần).

In these songs, the buffalo is depicted as an animal with a customarily gentle and hardworking nature. Similarly, in many Vietnamese proverbs too, the buffalo is uniformly depicted as an animal with remarkable strength and endurance:

- 'Usually, I'm as strong as a buffalo but these days whenever I go home, I just lie down' (*mọi hôm khoẻ như trâu ấy, mà nay về nhà cứ nằm dài thườn thượt*).

- 'Even the sick buffalo is stronger than a strong cow' *(trâu he cũng bằng bò khỏe).*
- 'Working crazy hard like a buffalo' *(làm như trâu điên).*
- 'As aggressive as a rolling buffalo' *(hùng hục như trâu lăn).*
- 'That guy is a real buffalo'—referring to those who are strong and vigorous.[12]

The ancient lyrics taught in schools, and the proverbs, mentioned above, indicate that the buffalo has long been the symbol of peace and prosperity in the cultural imaginary of the nation, a peace that in reality has eluded the Vietnamese for centuries.[13]

Different to this harmonious human-animal bondage, the human-animal binary is identifiable elsewhere in Vietnamese culture. Pervasively in various literatures, the animal world, conceived as the realm of the uncivilized, is recorded. As K.W. Taylor identifies, early nation-building legends of Vietnam include stories about the boundary between the realms of human beings and animals, in which the former stands for civilization and the latter for the uncivilized world: this clearly appears to be anthropocentric. The first of these early legends is about the beautiful snakes in Mê Linh district, where Hùng King, a descendent of the Dragon, traditionally held to be the progenitor of the Vietnamese people, once ruled. The second story is about

---

[12] Nguyễn Văn Trào, ibid. 97

[13] Catherine Noppe and Jean-François Hubert. *Art of Vietnam.* Parkstone International, 2018, 307.

the chimpanzees in Cổ Loa, the capital city until the tenth century. The third story is about a tiger in Luy Lâu, the administrative center of the Hán emperor, located thirty kilometres away from Hanoi, the present-day capital. The main point of these stories appears to be to dramatically reveal how royal kings control or even destroy animals, who become a hindrance to the process of civilizing the local people and ruling them.[14] As such, the animals stand for the power of nature and signify destruction, rebellion and savagery as opposed to civilized society. Not only in legends but also in folk tales, animals are depicted as uncivilized beings, bearing characteristics associated with savagery. For example, in many proverbs, dogs are portrayed in very negative ways, as evil, insolent, fierce or stupid. This can easily be clearly illustrated by identifying idiomatic phrases where the term 'dog' forms an element. For example:

- Dirty like a dog (*bẩn như chó*).
- Stupid like a dog (*ngu như chó*).
- Eat [greedily] like a dog (*ăn như chó*).
- Black [bad luck] like a dog (*đen như chó*).
- Insolent like a dog (*hỗn như chó*).
- An insincere flatterer like a dog (*nịnh như chó*).
- Such a dead-dog day (*ngày chó chết*)—referring to an unlucky day.
- Sad like a sick dog (*buồn như chó ốm*).

---

[14] K.W. Taylor. *A History of the Vietnamese*. Cambridge University Press, 2013.

These phrases attest to the negative connotations that surround dogs. There are many other examples that could be added to this list to show that Vietnamese people often have a negative attitude towards dogs.[15] Therefore, it is fair to say that in Vietnamese culture, the animal constitutes a symbol of the opposing or destructive force that combats the supposedly civilized human society.

As a consequence of this, animals in Vietnamese literature and culture came to be associated with characters or things that carried negative connotations. For example, in most Vietnamese cultures, there is a belief that the owl is a bad omen, a symbol of disaster and death. In addition, owls are also seen as ugly. Proverbs and phrases that make such references abound:

- 'How is an owl in a match with a fairy?'.
- 'Foul like an owl'
- 'On opening the shop this morning, I saw an owl. It's sure to be a bad sales day!'.[16]

Many people also believe that if snakes or wild animals enter their home, it does not augur well for them.[17] On the first day of the lunar new year, if the first sound you hear is a cock crow, then it 'portends bad crops'; if it's the

---

[15] Read. Nguyễn Văn Trào. Ibid, 95.

[16] Nguyễn Ngọc Trào, Ibid, 96.

[17] La Công Ý. 'The Perilous Journey of the *Then* Spirit Armey: A Shamanic Ritual of the Tay People'. *Vietnam: Journeys of Body, Mind, and Spirit*. Ed. Van Huy Nguyen, Laurel Kendall. University of California Press, 2003, pp. 238–251.

buffalo you hear, it's 'a toilsome year ahead'.[18] Therefore, in the Vietnamese cultural imaginary, animals inhabit a superstitious, irrational realm. They are not given either autonomy or agency. They appear to be merely portents placed to warn human beings. Indeed, therefore, in a very real sense, as Donna Harraway observes, 'animals are the mirrors that we polish to look for ourselves.'[19]

Animal Studies and Ecocriticism in Vietnam

It is against this background that ecological criticism emerged in Vietnam in early 2010,[20] when the relationship that tradition had entrenched between humans and animals was questioned. In other words, ecocritics in Vietnam began reading their cultural literature with insight about the noticeable absence of the representation of animal agency. As a consequence, attempts were made to redress this. For example, Tran Ngoc Hieu and Dang Thai Ha (2017) strive to excavate animal voices in post-war (post-1975) Vietnamese narratives. They observe that in the preceding war narratives, the absence of animal agency can be seen as symptomatic of the revolutionary anti-colonial struggle, where all individual voices—both animal and human—were suppressed and subsumed within the singular voice that spoke about and strengthened the nation's anti-colonial struggle. Interestingly, the two

---

[18] Vietnam. Bộ Ngoại giao. *An Introduction to Vietnam*. Embassy of Vietnam, 1969.

[19] Quoted above.

[20] Chi Pham and Chitra Sankaran, *Revenge of Gaia: Contemporary Vietnamese Ecofiction*. Random Penguin House, 2021, 1–6.

critics, Tran and Dang, read the image of the human-ape in Bảo Ninh's *The Sorrow of War* (1990) as a metaphor for animals' demand that their past tragedies and sufferings during the time of war be finally recognized.[21] In a similar vein, ecocritics, Trần Thị Ánh Nguyệt and Lê Lưu Oanh (2016) point out that much of contemporary Vietnamese ecofiction aims to provoke the public into a rude awakening about the unfair treatment that has been meted out to non-human nature—including animals—during the war when they were enthusiastically exploited as merely a form of natural resource to support the national struggle against American imperialism. The aim of this body of literature appears to mainly be consciousness-raising. It attempts to foreground the cruelty that is endemic to animal treatment in Vietnamese society. Instead, it places emphasis on attributes such as love and respect for animals, and the protection of all species as a foundational principle. Thus, we find that in this literature, animals force humans to abandon their conventionally held notion of human exclusivity and instead persuade humankind to acknowledge the equal status of animals and indeed, to respect the rights owed to non-human nature in its diverse forms. Noticeably, these two female ecocritics, Tran and Le, highlight how the animals' perspectives are centered in

---

[21] Tran Ngoc Hieu, and Dang Thai Ha. 'Listening to Nature, Rethinking the Past: A Reading of the Representations of Forests and Rivers in Post-war Vietnamese Narratives.' *Southeast Asian Ecocriticism: Theories, Practices, Prospects*, edited by John Charles Ryan. Lexington Books, 2018, pp. 205–228.

short stories such as, 'Facing Up Once' (1982)[22]and 'Giát Market Day' (1986)[23] by the famous author, Nguyễn Minh Châu. In these stories, human lives are recounted through the lens of a cat and a buffalo, respectively; these lenses go beyond any clichéd invoking of animals through an anthropocentric lens. Instead, these animal characters leap out of the pages, speaking with autonomy and agency.

Vietnamese ecocritics are therefore exploring how in contemporary literary works, animals are not used merely as metaphors that reflect aspects of the human but, on the contrary, in many instances, animals are depicted as autonomous agents in themselves. Animals are shown to engage with and actively influence narrative plot and flow. More specifically, these ecocritics attempt to find in local animal stories, themes and patterns that 'Animal Studies' scholars discover in *global* animal narratives elsewhere. For example, the central character, the dog, Bi, in the novel *Chó Bi, đời lưu lạc* (*The Dog Bi, a Wandering Life*) by Ma Văn Kháng (2006) is conventionally read as a metaphor for 'beauty' in human society. The wandering life of the dog is typically read as representative of the life of a righteous human being, who is 'born in tragedy, in pain and in squalor though possessing self-confidence and pride.'[24] As a book review contends, Bi's string of tragedies and

---

[22] English version is in *Revenge of Gaya: Contemporary Vietnamese Ecofiction* (Chi P. Pham and Chitra Sankarna), Penguin Random House, 2021.

[23] This story is translated in this collection.

[24] Fahasa Book Store. https://www.fahasa.com/cho-bi-doi-luu-lac-tai-ban-2016.html. Accessed March 7, 2023.

wandering functions like beads that 'connect through the thread of social relationships,'[25] all standing for people who are 'miserable and unhappy but still yearn to rise up with intense vitality'[26]. As such, the dog, Bi, still functions as a metaphor.

With the new, ecocritical approach, however, Nguyễn Thùy Trang (2018) reads the dog, Bi, in this novel as an autonomous being, who has the power to ravenge himself against humankind if he is bullied or abused. Although the older ways of reading animals as cultural symbols remain, the new ecocritical lesson learnt appears to be to challenge and reverse traditional anthropocentric perspectives such as are highlighted in the popular Vietnamese proverb: 'people are flowers of the earth' (*người ta là hoa đất*). Instead, Nguyễn argues that in the narrative, Bi signifies the victory of the 'Other' over the 'human', thus counteracting anthropocentrism. She claims that these animal portrayals shift agency from humans to animals. They satirize and negate humankind's confidence in its ability to dominate the world at large and control non-human beings in particular.[27]

Thinking about animal narratives from the perspective of ecocriticism has made Vietnamese scholars more active in their search for animal voices and subjects in literary texts. However, this has exposed a deep ambivalence and

---

[25] Fahasa Book Store. https://www.fahasa.com/cho-bi-doi-luu-lac-tai-ban-2016.html. Accessed March 7, 2023.

[26] Fahasa Book Store. https://www.fahasa.com/cho-bi-doi-luu-lac-tai-ban-2016.html. Accessed March 7, 2023.

[27] Nguyễn Thùy Trang. *Tiểu thuyết Việt Nam giai đoạn 1986–2014 từ góc nhìn phê bình sinh thái*. Dissertation. Hue University of Education, 2018.

an unresolved binary in the way animals have impacted Vietnamese culture and literature. While on the one hand, an aspect of their culture leads them to respect and love animals, on the other, the sense that animals are a source of labour or food persists. They realize that this strangely contradictory sentiment arises due to contrary ideological influences. The former sentiment is due to ancient philosophies from India and China, whose impulse is to stress the continuum between non-human nature and humankind, that forms the fabric of the traditional Vietnamese faith-systems. More recently, this has been reinforced by the introduction of ecocritical theory, and environmental and animal movements in academic and educational life since the early years of the twenty-first century, which also seek to elevate the status of animals and grant them autonomy. However, opposed to this is the impulse to objectify non-human nature. The latter is also part of Vietnamese cultural tradition, and is due to the influence of Marxist materialism in Vietnam's economic and political life, which encourages the view of the natural world as a production source for the nation's modernization.

Ecocritics, seeking out their ancient cultural roots, look to the influence of Eastern philosophies. These have acted as stimuli for Vietnamese scholars to return to their ancient beliefs to seek a response to Western ecological theory. In this return to roots, Vietnamese ecological critics emphasize the philosophical precept of living in harmony with nature as the highest wisdom imbibed by man. A prominent scholar who advocates this line of thought is Nguyễn Tịnh Thy, a leading Vietnamese ecocritic. She borrows the philosophy of Lao Tzu to approach three famous animal stories of the writer Trần Duy Phiên: 'Man and Termite', 'Ant and Man', and 'Spider and Man'[28]. According to this critic, the fury of the animal world as well as the painful defeat of humans reinforces the fact that in modern, industrialized society, we live in disharmony with nature. These fictions focus on the fact that humans routinely encroach upon and appropriate the habitat of animals. This is interpreted as a violation of Lao Tzu's philosophy of 'not doing', a philosophy, which, as explained by the ecocritic, Nguyễn Tịnh Thy, advocates that human beings should do nothing contrary to the law of nature and hence proceed to do everything to coexist in harmony with nature.[29] In this context, the term '*mơ hồ sinh thái*' (ecological ambiguity), which is widely believed among Vietnamese ecocritics to derive from Karen Thornber's ecoambiguity (2015), is perceived by Vietnamese ecocritics as accurately reflecting their cultural dilemma. In an interview, green humanities scholar, Nguyễn Đăng Điệp, Director of Institute of Literature (Vietnam Academy of Social Sciences) (2016) observes that

> Vietnamese people love animals but are willing to eat meat. We build a park, but to build it, we must sacrifice other creatures to create our park. Thus, in our development, hesitation and ambivalence are very evident.[30]

---

[28] English versions are in *Revenge of Gaia*, Ibid.

[29] Nguyễn Tịnh Thy. *Rừng khô, suối cạn, biển độc . . . và văn chương*. Hà Nội: Khoa học Xã hội Press, 2017: 287–302.

[30] Nguyễn Đăng Điệp. Chúng ta yêu động vật, nhưng sẵn sàng ăn thịt chúng. Interviewed by Thu Hiền. *Thanh niên* December, 16, 2017. Accessed March 17, 2023. https://zingnews.vn/chung-ta-yeu-dong-vat-nhung-san-sang-an-thit-chung-post804276.html

His statement reveals that Thornber's ecoambiguity is acknowledged as central to the way in which the Vietnamese perceive their relationship with nonhuman nature. The first sentence reflects a sentiment that has had wide circulation among ecocritics: 'Vietnamese people love the dog but they still eat it'. The director's interview presents the consensus of opinion among Vietnamese ecological critics about a contradiction; an inconsistency in human's attitude and behaviour towards animals. Or to put it differently, in Vietnam, a reverence for nature and a sense of harmony with it is simultaneously held along with its objectification. So, in this sense, this term accurately reveals the indeterminate feeling that Vietnamese culture projects towards animals and non-human nature.

An Analysis of the Current Selection of Animal Fiction

Most scholars of animal fiction point out that traditional animal narratives are more about humans than animals. They assert that the animals in the stories are anthropomorphized, therefore reflecting more about human lives than about animal communities, which remain as obscure as ever. This leads to anthropocentrism. As Fiona Probyn-Rapsey clarifies, 'Anthropocentrism refers to a form of human centeredness that places humans not only at the center of everything but makes "us" the most important measure of all things.'[31] However, the short stories in this collection can be described as challenging and countering

---

[31] Fiona Probyn-Rapsey. 'Anthropocentrism.' In L. Gruen (Ed.), *Critical Terms for Animal Studies*. Chicago, United States: University of Chicago Press, 2018, pp. 47.

anthropocentrism in a multitude of ways. Though one might argue that the narrative lens in some cases appears to emerge from the human perspective and to focus on human predicaments, several of these narratives also decent the human in significant ways. Indeed, anthropocentrism is deeply critiqued and challenged in this volume in a variety of ways. The human world is presented as imperfect and deeply flawed and the lens through which this is articulated in several stories is the animals. Furthermore, the humans that populate this world are shown as inferior to the animal characters, firmly challenging the human/animal value-dualism. This occurs in practically every story. In 'Crossing the Forest to Save Younger Sister', Minh's sister, Thu, is kidnapped by organ traffickers. On his way through the forest to track her, Minh is joined at various stages of his journey by his animal friends. We come to learn that all the animals that join Minh in his rescue mission are victims of human abuse. As they help Minh search for his sister, they come across many fiendish human acts and try to rectify these. For example, they destroy a poppy field they discover in the middle of a forest. The flawed humans and their egocentric worldviews are constantly held up for scrutiny. In 'Raw Fish', the greedy uncle of the narrator, who endlessly devours fish caught by his brother to satiate his appetite, is finally eaten up by a giant fish. There is a satisfactory sense of natural justice that demotes human exclusivity and brings humankind within the sphere of a *dharmic* (righteous) natural order.

In 'Ants Pursue Their Own Direction', human cruelty towards insects is clearly challenged and indicted. The ants in the house pursue their lives and their work without causing any problems to the humans. 'A swarm of fire-ants leisurely made their way in and out of every little crevice and fissure.' But to the woman who has entered her boyfriend's house, their very presence becomes an intolerable menace. This sense of oppression grows on her until, the following day, when they are setting out on a picnic:

> She deliberately lingered, waiting for [her boyfriend] to disappear. Then, she hastily rummaged through his store room to look for the ant spray that she had hidden earlier and began spraying . . . under the stove, near the door . . . everywhere. She covered her nose, closed her eyes, and sprayed. A pungent smell rose into the air. She dashed to the door and shut it deftly behind her. She turned the lock twice. Her face was pale like a thief caught in the act. She threw the spray in a public trash can and went in search of him.

This dreadful, illogical, mass extermination exposes the entitlement that is innate to the urbanized human being. They believe that no other life form on this planet has the right to its own space, even if it does not get in the way of humans. It also shows how such insane acts, which, if perpetrated on other humans would be tantamount to terrorism, has been normalized in human society, thus revealing how human exclusivity and speciesism are so entrenched that they are never challenged. Her cruelty to the ants is, however, the point of no return for the boyfriend. He decides to terminate their relationship.

'In the Editing Room' links two important ideas: the anthropocentric legacy, wherein only humans are deemed to have any intrinsic value as a species, conjoined with the idea of how laughable it is to believe that humans live above their instinctual animality. Even as the junior proof-reader is pondering whether dragonflies are capable of thought or emotion or live only by unthinking instinct, the editor is secretly obsessing over her breasts and wondering why he is unable to divert his attention. The juxtaposing of these two lines of thought reveals how humans are as enslaved by their basic instincts as any dragonfly, and it is laughable that they claim superiority over the animal by measure of their reason and intellect.

One of the most moving and subtle narrations that reveal the sad, confused, human world and its distorted values, and humanity's helpless entanglement with the animal kingdom is 'Market Day in Giát District'. Old man Khúng, old, feeble, and after a lifetime of brutal labour has finally decided that it is now time to sell his lifetime companion, his beloved ox, which had toiled with him for several decades and was more a member of the family than a 'mute brute', to the butchers. His recollection of their shared life torments him until he finally decides to let the ox free to spend its last days in the wild. The irony is that when he finally turns up in his daughter's residence, it is to find the loyal ox waiting there for him.

> The ox looked up at the old man with eyes that looked sorrowful and filled with longing. It was the look of a creature which had returned willingly, accepting its fate. Standing silently next to his loaded cart, which he had toiled to pull all the way, Khúng didn't know how to react to the animal's presence. He couldn't bring himself to blame the animal, so he just gazed at this old friend, his close business partner with eyes that were filled with deep sadness.

This deep bond between man and animal is also the central theme in 'Old Hac'. Here, the old man decides to commit suicide after the loss of his beloved dog and son, both equally cherished and loved. The narrative also lends insight into the socio-economic privations that elderly, impoverished people face in Vietnamese society. The old man is forced to sell his dog and this is the main cause of his distress. The story is also valuable for the details it provides regarding the cultural practice of baiting and killing dogs, in order to cure the meat and prepare *galangal* (a herb-based) dog meat.

Another way in which this collection speaks to modern, emergent perspectives in Animal Studies is through making a space for the voices of animals to be heard in ways that are not subsumed by the human. In 'Crossing the Forest to Save Younger Sister', for example, Minh's animal friends are all autonomous entities with histories that speak of their sad encounters with humans. The animals vividly recount their tales of abuse and brutality in the hands of their human 'masters'. At the end of the story, they request Minh to establish a shelter for abused animals. Similarly, in 'Ants Pursue Their Own Direction', the final telling comment rests with the fate of the ants, so brutally killed by the young woman. The man reflects:

> Ants don't take up much space. They have been around for millions of years but unlike humans, they did not endlessly proliferate, annexing more and more of the planet's spaces, fighting with each other . . . trampling over others. He dreaded the thought of having a family with her . . .

These lines assert the uneven balance between humans and other life forms. Human predatoriness and cruelty, and the complete vulnerability of non-human animals are compellingly brought home to the reader in this story. But interestingly, in 'Tiger Smell', the agency of the animal is forcefully reinforced. This story also emphasizes the ancient and pervasive belief in *Karma* theory: that one has to pay the price for exploiting nature and using it in utilitarian ways. This is graphically illustrated when the protagonist, a circus artist, who trains and controls a tiger to earn her livelihood, finally dies in its clutches, paying her karmic price.

This theme of animal agency is a very strong thread that runs through the stories, challenging and reversing anthropocentrism. In 'Love Letter' the human-animal continuum is presented unproblematically. The author, steps into the pages of his narrative to assert animal agency in an interesting stylistic manoeuver:

> I, the author who penned this story, know another truth. I cannot help wondering why that day, Đoàn's family dog approached his master's table, looked around, and then leaning forward, he moved his front paw and took hold of a pen to write on the leather. It wrote most vigorously and energetically letting out an occasional frenetic howl. After a brief stint of writing, the dog appeared to lose steam. It appeared bitter. Pulling its tail tight, it laid its muzzle on the broom handle. Closing its eyes, it lay in contemplation all afternoon.

He leaves speculation rife as to who the instigator of the events that led to the downfall of the family actually is.

Indeed, the agency of animals is surfaced in various ways in these stories. Fantasy and reality mingle to create a world where all possibilities co-exist and animals are forcibly brought into the human fold demanding recognition and respect. In 'Rose Villa', we find reality and fantasy mingle without problem when the real world of a young protagonist, Lam, seamlessly flows into a fantasy world when he climbs a gate and enters a fecund natural world where all animals live in amity. The young girl that the protagonist meets, An, seems an embodiment of mother nature. These stories open up a world where the strong binary between human and animal is effectively subverted, leaving the suggestion that humans and animals exist in a continuum that forms the vast web of life on earth.

In conclusion, this collection is a valuable resource that reveals the complex mosaic of human-animal interaction in Vietnamese culture.

Bibliography

Anonymous. https://www.fahasa.com/cho-bi-doi-luu-lac-tai-ban-2016.html. *Fahasa Book Store*. Accessed March 7, 2023.

American Institutes for Research Headquarters. *Minority Groups in North Vietnam*, Department of the Army, 1972, pp. 271–277.

Derrida, Jacques and David Wills. 'The Animal That Therefore I Am (More to Follow)', *Critical Inquiry*, Vol. 28, No. 2, Winter, 2002, pp. 369–418.

Dutton, George Edson, Jayne Susan Werner, John K. Whitmore. *Sources of Vietnamese Tradition*. Translated and Edited by Columbia University Press, 2012.

Haraway, Donna. *Simians, Cyborgs, and Women: The Reinvention of Nature*. New York: Routledge, 1991.

La Công Ý. 'The Perilous Journey of the *Then* Spirit Armey: A Shamanic Ritual of the Tay People'. *Vietnam: Journeys of Body, Mind, and Spirit*. Ed. Van Huy Nguyen, Laurel Kendall. University of California Press, 2003.

Nguyễn Đăng Điệp. Chúng ta yêu động vật, nhưng sẵn sàng ăn thịt chúng. Interviewed by Thu Hiền. *Thanh niên* 16.12.2017. Accessed March 17, 2023. https://zingnews.vn/chung-ta-yeu-dong-vat-nhung-san-sang-an-thit-chung-post804276.html

Nguyễn Thùy Trang. *Tiểu thuyết Việt Nam giai đoạn 1986–2014 từ góc nhìn phê bình sinh thái*. Dissertation. Hue University of Education, 2018.

Nguyễn Tịnh Thy. *Rừng khô, suối cạn, biển độc... và văn chương*. Hà Nội: Khoa học Xã hội Press, 2017, pp. 287–302.

Nguyễn Văn Trào. 'Nghĩa biểu trưng văn hóa của các từ chỉ động vật trong tiếng Anh và tiếng Việt'. Tạp chí *Khoa học xã hội Việt Nam*, số 4(77), 2014, pp. 93–103.

Noppe, Catherine and Jean-François Hubert. *Art of Vietnam*. Parkstone International, 2018, pp. 307.

Pham, Chi and Chitra Sankaran, *Revenge of Gaia: Contemporary Vietnamese Ecofiction*. Penguin Random House SEA, 2021.

Probyn-Rapsey, Fiona. (2018). 'Anthropocentrism.' In L. Gruen (Ed.), *Critical Terms for Animal Studies*. Chicago, United States: University of Chicago Press. 2021, pp. 47–63.

Sax, Boria. 'What is this quintessence of dust? The concept of the "human" and its origins.' In Rob Boddice (Ed.) *Anthropocentrism: Human, Animals, Environments*. Leiden, Boston: Brill. 2011.

Singer, Peter. *Animal Liberation: A New Ethics for Our Treatment of Animals*. New York: Harper Collins, 1975.

Taylor, K. W. *A History of the Vietnamese*. Cambridge University Press, 2013.

Tran, Ngoc Hieu, and Dang Thai Ha. 'Listening to Nature, Rethinking the Past: A Reading of the Representations of Forests and Rivers in Post-war Vietnamese Narratives.' *Southeast Asian Ecocriticism: Theories, Practices, Prospects*, edited by John Charles Ryan. Lexington Books, 2018, pp. 205–228.

Vietnam (Ministry of Foreign Affairs). *An Introduction to Vietnam*. Embassy of Vietnam Publication, 1969.

Author's Note

Please note that not all stories in this anthology have been translated in their entirety. There could be sections/ parts that have not been translated to English and thus do not appear in this book. All such sections are denoted by an ellipsis within brackets, like so [...].

'Con trâu' by Khương Hương

Crossing the Forest to Save Younger Sister (2021)

Y. Ban (1961)

1

Minh was planning to follow his mother to the farmstead. It was quite a long way off, so they had to traverse through three high mountains to reach it. Mother woke up early to cook *mèn mén* (corn rice). The scent of the corn rice was enough to lure Minh out of bed. There was no need for his mother to wake him up. Mother put the tray of mèn mén in front of Minh.

'Eat quickly and follow me out of the gate, otherwise the strong sunlight will scramble your brain.'

Mother wiped Minh's mouth and ate the rest of the mèn mén as she hastily stuffed things into her *mocuck*. Mother wrapped two portions of mèn mén in fresh banana leaves and packed it along with a bottle of water.

Minh ate but was so drowsy that he banged his head against the table. Mother took Minh's ear between her fingers sternly.

'Let's go!' she urged.

The sky was still dark. Minh followed his mother's shadow. Early morning dew blew on his cold face and dispelled his drowsiness. Mother turned to Minh.

'Don't fall down,' she warned.

Then his mother sang in a warm, loud voice:

'The rooster crowed in the morning, oh my dear, the rooster crowed in the morning.

The sun rises early, so wake up, it's already morning.

It's already morning in the forest and fields, my dear.'

Minh mumbled to himself, 'my stomach is happy' and sang along with his mother. Mother sang only one song but she sang it over and over again. Mother sang fluently in the national language (Kinh) without any problems. Minh suddenly realized that his mother's use of Kinh was very precise. She must have studied very well in the past. Before Minh was born, she used to be a teacher. Absorbed in his thoughts, Minh dropped behind. Suddenly he heard a very light flap of wings, and the chirping of a bird at dawn. Another bird responded sweetly and a choir of sweet bird notes rose in the air. Minh stood dazed as if his feet had become rooted to the ground, looking up to listen to the birdsong. How wonderful! This was so enchanting! His mind was giddy with excitement and his heart was thumping. Minh was supremely happy and shouted out:

'Please sing again, forest birds!'

He kept shouting aloud to the birds to continue their melody, totally absorbed in the morning-song until he was brought back to earth by his mother's voice:

'Minh, hurry up!'

Minh quickly caught up with his mother. Mother waited until he closed the distance between them and then turned again to hurry on. Minh looked up to gaze at his mother's back but only saw the mocuck. With his head bent, Minh followed his mother's footsteps. He wondered as he followed, *Why is she looking down? We all know that the earth never sleeps and doesn't need waking up. Why isn't she gazing up at the sky?*

Engrossed in the sky above, Minh lost his footing. His feet had got entangled in the bushes underfoot. Mother turned and pulled him up. 'Walk properly. Do not look up at the sky anymore. Look down at your feet and walk carefully. And hurry up! Otherwise, the sunlight will seep into your head.'

Minh did not dare to lift his eyes to the canopy of trees. He had to focus constantly while climbing uphill. It was not a gentle slope. The steep face of the rocky mountain almost touched his nose. Since Minh's feet were still short, he had to hold tightly to the vines and swing to climb. Mother was climbing sturdily ahead of him. She dropped the vines for Minh to hold and climb. However, both mother and son were still not stretched.

His father had explained to Minh that it was good to expand the lungs by panting. That way, the lungs were full of air and light. When Minh swung with all his strength to manage the steep slopes, he felt his lungs expanding. Then they felt light. He thought, *No wonder the corn baskets my parents carry home from the farm are so heavy! The corn has no lungs.*

'Now, let's sit down and rest for a while,' his mother said, pointing to a flat stone under a large tree that looked like a table in the village head's house.

Minh lay sprawled with his arms and legs spread wide. He felt refreshed. The shirt he was wearing was soaked with sweat and felt cool, pressed against the ice-cold stone.

'Mother, you lie down and rest too.'

'No. It's hard to get up after lying down, better to just sit.'

'Can I close my eyes and sleep for a bit?'

'Don't sleep, otherwise you won't be able to wake up later. It is better to reach the farmstead and then sleep.'

When the corn was piled high, as tall as a tree, Minh's eyes could no longer stay open. He crawled up the stairs and collapsed on the floor. Sleep caught him in its coils.

2

'Minh, wake up.'

A drop of cold water fell on Minh's hot cheeks. Sleep had trapped him in its coils for too long. He only woke up when the cold drops of water fell on his cheeks. Minh opened his eyes and sat up quickly when he observed his mother's eyes filled with pain.

'Mother, what's happened to you?'

Please run quickly back to the village and fetch your father'.

'Why mother, what's wrong?'

Minh felt as though his stomach had turned upside down. His mother's face was so pale. He had never seen her look so pale before.

'I'm fine now, my boy. I'm not even bleeding anymore. I was just so unlucky today. My knife sliced my leg instead of the tree. See.' Only then did Minh look down at his mother's leg. Mother's headscarf was wrapped tightly around her ankles, which had changed from ivory white to red. Minh hugged his mother and sobbed. Mom also hugged Minh tightly back. This was unusual for her. Mother did not usually encourage such emotional overtures. When he had tried to hug her before, she'd always reprimanded him saying, 'such emotional displays will weaken you.' Now, his mother held him tightly before pushing him away, very deliberately.

'Son, wipe your tears. You will have to go home alone. It's a long way. You need to leave early or it will get dark and you'll lose your way. I have packed some water and the rest of the mèn mén into the mocuck. Now, sling it around your neck. When you are hungry or thirsty, make sure you sit down and eat.'

'I'm not hungry. You need to eat more than me. You have lost a lot of blood and you still haven't eaten anything. I already ate my portion.' he protested. But mother said, 'Don't argue with me anymore, hurry up.'

Mother put a blanket around Minh's neck, pushed him down the stairs and went back upstairs. Minh halted after a while. He was determined not to eat his mother's mèn mén portion. He thought about how from dawn until now, his mother has not eaten anything. She had worked non-stop while he had just slept. With his mind made up, he turned back and crept up the stairs. Mother had fallen asleep leaning against the piled-up corn. Minh left the mèn mén packet and the water bottle next to his mother. He wanted so much to hug her again but was afraid of waking her up. He wiped his tears with his knuckles and tiptoed down the stairs [. . .]

[. . .] Minh's house was one of the few located near the stream. Minh's father was a member of the village committee. He had so wanted his family to move to the city to engage in the various entertainments offered there and also to reduce his commute time. But his mother was reluctant. Since father heeded mother's words, he had not pressed for the move.

Minh's house always had a surplus of corn which they could not consume. Mother worked hard in the field. Minh had heard his father say many times to his mother, 'You don't have to go to the fields. You can stay at home to grow vegetables and raise chickens.' His mother would respond with, 'But I have fun working in the field.'

Minh's parents addressed each other as 'anh' and 'em', which actually translated into 'older brother' and 'younger sister'. This was because they spoke in Mandarin unlike the rest of the villagers who rarely spoke in this mainstream lingo. Father had once explained to Minh: 'Your mother used to be my teacher' to which Minh had teasingly retorted, 'then why don't you fold your arms respectfully every time you address her'.

Hearing his cheeky retort, his parents would laugh and exchange glances. When grandma was still alive, she used to urge Minh's mother to have more children for she believed that children were akin to wealth. Therefore, more children meant that the family was more fortunate. Minh's mother would smile and agree. 'Sure!' she would say, 'I'll produce more siblings for Minh.' However, his father was not for this. He only allowed his mother to give birth to one more child, Thu. His father felt that raising many children would be hard on his mother.

3

The sun was rising gradually reaching the zenith of the mountain ahead. Minh did not have the patience to follow the usual path home. He decided to take a shortcut down the stream. The cool water felt blissful. It would have been heavenly to take off his clothes and plunge into the water. But he didn't have the time. His mother was lying in the farmstead in acute pain. He didn't yield to his temptation to play with the water, he was focused on getting home fast.

Suddenly, he spied four men at a distance, walking along the stream. They were walking briskly. One of them was carrying a large sack on his back. That was strange! There were hardly any strangers in this village. Whose house were they visiting? His? Or were they going to Uncle A Tráng's house? Or were they going to Mr Phử house? He intuitively felt that these people were not good. He must inform his father.

However, Minh was still very preoccupied with his mother's condition. He really couldn't spare the time to think of these men. His only wish was that his father was already home so that he could rush to the farmstead to pick up mother. When Minh reached home, the sun was already setting. It was disappearing behind the mountains to retire for the day. Thu was nowhere to be seen. Perhaps she was still busy playing. If she had come home, she would have been jumping around in the front yard. His mother often remarked that Thu had wheels on her feet. But wait . . . why was the front door wide open? If father had returned from his office, his motorbike would have been parked in the front yard. There was something wrong and it worried Minh. He called out—

'Father, are you back yet?' There was silence. He called out again, 'Thu, sister Thu!'

Again, no one answered. Minh rushed into the house. It was dark inside and he could not see clearly. He stood still for a moment to get his bearings. After a moment of calm, he could see everything. Tables and chairs had been toppled. Both Thu's and his study tables were lying upside down. He caught sight of one of his sister's red sandals lying on the doorstep. Minh's heart was pounding. In his mind's eye, he saw the four men with a large sack hurrying along the stream. *Oh my God! Thu has been kidnapped*, he realized. He was paralysed with fear but managed to run like a madman to the stream, wading through the waters like one possessed [. . .]

6[32]

[. . .] Vines wrapped themselves tightly around Minh's ankles. He felt as though they were pulling him to the

---

[32] In chapters 4 and 5, Minh learns that it is the four men that he had met on the way home had kidnapped his sister. He decides to follow those men to rescue her.

ground. A tree branch lashed against his face. This hurt so much that he couldn't get up for some time. He muttered aloud, *I need to pay attention to the path ahead and must stop day-dreaming while walking.* When he scrutinized the ground, he realized that he could discern footprints of people who had walked before him. This made him happy. He assumed that Thu's kidnappers had passed here not too long ago since creepers, maggots and grasses were flattened out. Because of this, his path was smoother.

When he was not preoccupied by memories from before, he felt hunger pangs and his stomach rumbled. He felt his eyes dimming with fatigue. He tried to keep it open but a hundred fireflies appeared to dance before him. His knees trembled with exhaustion. He tried taking a few steps forward but then stumbled and fell, and felt his eyes closing.

'Hek hek . . .' He heard the chatter of monkeys and smelt the strong aroma of ripe guavas. This brought him back to his senses. Minh opened his eyes in bewilderment. A yellow-hued monkey was sticking a guava into Minh's face. Minh grabbed the fruit and ate it greedily. The monkey kept supplying Minh with more and more fruit . . . almost nine guavas. Minh only stopped to breathe. He ate continuously to assuage his intense hunger. The monkey grunted and then quickly jumped back up to the tree again. It continued to throw down ripe guavas from the tree.

Once his stomach was full, Minh lay still for a while longer to stave off the fatigue. When he finally sat up, he noticed that all around him lay a whole lot of ripe guavas. He laughed, 'Are you picking guavas to feed me, monkey? I thank you but I have to go now.' Minh stuffed his pockets with the ripe guavas lying around him and started walking once again along the long forest path. After a while, he reached a flat stretch of land. He noticed some half-burnt wood and dry cinders. He reached out and touched the ashes and felt their warmth. He felt very hopeful, *Perhaps Thu's kidnappers stopped here to boil water. They can't have gone very far. These are adults, no doubt, but they have to carry not only Thu but also other necessary commodities like food and water. So, they can't move very fast. If I walk faster, I'll definitely catch up with them. But how can I save Thu? It will be one against four. They might even add me to their list of abductees. Then my poor parents would have lost both their children at one go. My mother will be very distraught and will cry all day long. I need to strategize. I need a plan.*

'Hek hek . . .' the golden monkey was still following Minh. It seemed to have found a bunch of ripe bananas and was now throwing the fruit, one by one, to Minh. Minh patted his shoulder and beckoned the monkey. 'Want to come down and take a ride with me?' The monkey only hesitated for a second. Then it jumped onto Minh's shoulder. As it rode on his shoulder, it squealed its delight aloud and the whole forest seemed to resound with its joyous cackle [. . .]

8[33]

[. . .] 'Hek hek'. The monkey's chatter woke Minh up. He wished that the monkey would speak human language. Perhaps it would then say, 'Minh, wake up. We have almost

---

[33] In Chapter 7, Minh encounters several frightening situations while going through the forest to save his sister with the help of the monkey and the dog.

reached the stream.' Minh opened his eyes and found the monkey standing by his shoulder. He noticed the dog nearby. Its furry feet were wet.

'Are we near the stream?' Minh asked the monkey.

'Hek hek. That's right.'

'Can you speak human language?'

'Hek hek. No, I can't speak human language. It is you who now seems to understand the language of animals.'

'How is it that I didn't understand anything on the first day?'

'Because there was no need to communicate yet. You kinda understood me.'

The monkey yawned. While Minh was chatting with the monkey, the dog barked.

'Stop making so much noise.' Minh admonished it. 'If you know where the stream is, go ahead. Lead the way.'

The dog wagged its tail and darted forward.

They were very clearly near the stream because with every step they took, the sound of the gurgling water became louder. Minh was so excited that his footsteps were rushed.

Here it was. Minh waded into the water and soaked his hot, tired feet in the cool stream. The dog also jumped into the water. He started diving excitedly. But the monkey was afraid of the water and perched precariously on a rock. After diving around for a while, the dog came panting back to Minh with a fish in its mouth. It wanted to show off its handiwork.

Minh caressed the dog. 'You're brilliant! Now eat.' But the dog still held the fish in its mouth gazing at him. Minh said, 'Eat please. I don't eat raw fish.'

But the dog still held the fish in its mouth without swallowing. Then Minh understood what it wanted. Taking the fish from its mouth, he held it back to the dog. 'You're so smart. I can't imagine what made you run away to the forest. Here, take this fish. It's yours.'

Grabbing the fish from Minh's hand, the dog ate it with fervour.

Suddenly, the golden monkey jumped up a tree frantically, squealing loudly in its tongue:

'Watch out, there's a bear! A bear!'

Minh swung around and was faced with a huge, black bear. His limbs stiffened in terror. He couldn't react. It was too late to lie still with his face down, playing dead. So, he had to sit still. Even if he had jumped into the stream, he would have died from choking on the water.

But the dog came to his rescue. It dived in and caught another fish. It jumped on to the shore and quickly left the fish there, and barked loudly. It stood sturdily between Minh and the bear. In fact, the dog even started a fight with the bear, forcing the bear to raise its paw as if in surrender. That's when Minh realized that the bear had lost one of its rear legs. The dog kept up its loud barking. Then the bear left. The golden monkey returned and jumped on to Minh's shoulder.

'Bow wow,' barked the dog. 'Monkey, you are such a coward.'

'Hek hek,' declared the monkey. 'We don't know how to fight.'

'Okay. That's enough', said Minh. 'Stop blaming each other.'

Minh followed the course of the stream. He wondered, *Why didn't I figure out that people have to follow the stream to make some headway. For one, they need water to survive.*

A little further on, Minh saw some half-burnt twigs. *My guess was right,* he thought. He shoveled aside the burnt twigs with his hands and found one still warm piece of coal. He felt elated and shouted out loud, 'Look, there's warmth in this fire that's died down.'

The monkey danced jubilantly and clapped its hands. Minh searched around for dry twigs and leaves. He carefully built a fire. He had been the first boy among the others in his village who was able to build a fire and had won every time there was a competition. When Lý, Thảo and he met after school was over, they each had only one match. The rule was that whoever could light a fire and stoke it, would win.

When the fire was crackling brightly, Minh ordered the dog to catch a fish for him. The dog raced back to the stream again. Meanwhile, Minh spied a fat crab inside a hole in the rock and deftly caught it. Minh arranged the burning embers and placed the crab on the make-shift grill. The aroma of the grilled crab made Minh drool so much that he had to wipe it with his hand. *Grilled crab! How delicious it tasted!* Minh couldn't resist eating it straight away despite it being so hot. The dog too had caught a fish. It came dashing up to Minh, spraying water everywhere.

'Ha Ha! You're brilliant! Here, have this.' Minh held out the crab shell to the dog. The dog began enthusiastically crunching the shell.

Next, Minh poked a sharp, sturdy twig all the way into the fish through its mouth. Then he threw some hot coal inside. The skewered fish had a strong smell that filled the air. He broke bits of it and called out to the monkey. 'Hek, come here and eat!'

When the golden monkey approached, Minh held out the fish to it. But the monkey turned away and covered its nose with its palm.

'Hek hek, fish is not for me.'

'Then let the dog and me eat.'

Minh sensed a visitor lurking in the bushes. He was not surprised. It was the amputee bear. Minh stood up holding out a piece of fish.

'Bear, come here! Have you ever eaten grilled fish before?'

The dog barked agitatedly.

'Come on, stop barking. The bear only wants to be our friend.'

The bear lurched out of the bush. Then, it went downstream and dipped its head in the waters and emerged with a very large fish in its mouth. It then brought the fish up to Minh and dropped it on the ground beside him. It then repeated this action. With the bear's cooperation, Minh and the dog enjoyed a fulsome meal of grilled fish.

9

Minh gathered stout branches and piled them up to build a fire. Stout, dry wood burnt longer. The dog, satiated with the fish, lay stretched out by the fire, half dozing, sometimes coming awake with a sudden jerk and barking loudly. It repeated this time and again. Minh put his hand on the dog and gently stroked it. The dog calmed down and went back to sleep. The bear was also lying close to the fire. It too was dozing. In the middle of its slumber, it suddenly growled as if it had had a bad dream and shook awake. It then sighed deeply and snoozed again. Monkey too was curled up beside Minh.

Only Minh was wide awake. He was worried about Thu. It had already been three days. He didn't know how she was. Was she ill, perhaps? *My dear sister, please don't fall ill. I'm coming to rescue you soon.*

Minh looked at the sleeping dog and wondered why its snout had this deep cleft. He then looked at the bear curious as to how it had come to lose a foreleg. The dog was in deep slumber, hiccupping a few times. Minh lay by the dog and hugged him tight.

'Sleep well. With me beside you, no one will dare hurt you. I promise'.

'Bow-wow, do you want to hear my story?'

'Tell me, dear dog. Telling the whole story will lighten your heart'.

'Bow wow . . . I'm a bulldog. My name is Tom and my brother's name is Terry. We were brought here from a farm in England. We were trained to herd sheep. We were barely two months old when we came to Vietnam. We were well taken care of by our owner. We were fed well and bathed every day. We played on a lush green lawn. At night, we even slept on a soft mattress. My brother and I were very happy and loved our master very much. Every time our master stroked me, I was filled with affection for him. So was my brother.

Then, one day, our master came home with a dog-trainer. My brother and I said to each other, "Our childhood days are now over. We are about to become full-fledged adults. This means that we need to learn new skills. We must both work hard to acquire these skills to be worthy of our kind master".

Having lived with our parents in a dog farm in England, we were aware of what a bulldog needed to learn. We had to memorize commands. Let me explain this to you. We got the name "bulldog" due to our strong resemblance to a bull. Our fierce and rugged appearance deceives people into thinking that we are very combative. But in actual fact, we are gentle and friendly. Also, I need to confess that we are rather lazy and averse to instructions. We just love to eat well, sleep and be pampered. We especially enjoy playing with babies. Because I recognized these traits in myself, I warned Terry, "We need to study hard. Our master has been kind to us. He didn't seem to mind how much money he had to spend in order to bring us here. On hot days, he even lets us lie down beside the cool air conditioners and on cold days, we are warmed by heaters".

"Right!" said Terry. "But stop being so sentimental."

At any rate, both of us prepared ourselves for serious study.

The trainer began his training by chaining me to a tree with a large chain. I was left to starve. I tried to lie still even though it was the very first time that I had ever been chained. I was alert, waiting to see and hear any signal that might come my way. Terry had not been chained. He was given a plate of delicious sausages. I craved the food and started drooling. I tried my best to lie quietly but it was impossible. I got up, barked loudly and pulled the chain so tight that I was almost strangled. I started getting angry. I jumped up and down. Finally, the trainer let me off the leash. I rushed to eat Terry's sausages. Terry was enjoying his food. When he sensed someone coming for it, he started growling. But when he recognized me, he left the rest of the meal for me since his stomach was full anyway. The following day, it was Terry's turn to be chained while I got to eat. I had learned from Terry to share my food with him.

The next day, Terry and I were left to starve the whole day. Then, I was chained and Terry was only allowed a small amount of food. When I was released, I rushed to eat the food. But this time, Terry fended me off fiercely. Both of us snarled and jumped at each other's throats. The trainer lashed us with his whip, accompanying this with loud, excited shouts. "Go on . . . you two . . . kill each other."

Gradually, the days we were starved nearly to death increased from one day to two, then three and finally to a week. When we were unleashed, instead of rushing to the plate of food, Terry and I rushed to bite each other. This continued for a while until the two of us no longer needed to be leashed at all, indeed, no longer even needed the plate of food to vent our bloodlust. We only had to listen to the trainer's loud command and we lunged at each other snarling and biting. He barked out, "Go on . . . kill each other" and the next moment, we were at each other's throats.

Once we had internalized this command, we were entered into dogfights. Terry and I no longer fought each other but against other opponents. At the end of each fight, our bodies were battered, ripped and bloody. Flies and mosquitoes buzzed around us hungry for our blood. This made our wounds even more painful, sore and itchy. Terry and I were getting good at the dogfights and we beat one opponent after another. My master collected a pile of money. After every win, we were fed well. We did our very best to serve our owner. But our animal instincts were also getting honed.

During one of those fights, I faced a deadly opponent, a Tibetan mastiff. It wrenched off half of my snout with one sharp bite. The pain was unbearable. I was agonized with it. I ran straight into the forest and that's where I met you.'

Tears streamed down the dog's face.

'I saw my reflection in the water when I went to catch fish in the stream. I looked frightful. I used to belong to one of the most majestic dog breeds in the world. But now, I look hideous. I don't want to live on like this'.

Minh's voice was gentle as he comforted the dog, 'Tom, you're still handsome. In fact, your broken snout looks sexy. Now just go to sleep. I wish you a restful sleep without nightmares. Remember, with me beside you, no one can bully you anymore. Now just get some rest, Tom.'

10

'Growl, I want to tell my story too. Is anyone willing to listen to me?'

Tom rushed in to comfort the bear. 'Please don't cry, my friend, tell all of us your story. I'm sorry that I barked at you at the stream, I was just afraid that you would attack Minh.'

'Can I come and lie down beside you, Tom?' The bear asked.

'Yeah, come here. You lie between Minh and me.' replied Tom.

The monkey interrupted, 'Hey, what about me? Where can I lie down?'

'You can lie on my back or the bear's back,' said Minh.

The bear began his sad tale. 'They built an iron cage and locked me inside. They cooked some tasteless mush and fed me with it. I couldn't bear to eat it at first. But everyday, they only brought this mush out at mealtimes. So, in the end, out of desperate hunger, I was forced to eat it. I struggled every day to live in that miserable cage. I missed the forest and my friends. It was not just me who was caged but there were ten other bears. We exchanged doleful glances through the iron bars. It went on day after day, endlessly, it seemed.

One day, our keepers brought in a machine, which they called an "ultrasound machine". They put some anesthetic in our food and knocked us out. Then they did an ultrasound on all of us to see if our gallbladders were bloated with water. They poked a needle through our skin and into our gallbladder to suck out the bile. When we woke up, we were all in a lot of pain because our bodies lacked bile. We became weak and tired. We couldn't eat or drink for a week.

This procedure was repeated every three months when our gallbladders were emptied of bile. Although we were in constant pain, our growth process continued. When I wanted to have a baby, they mated me with a male bear. I got pregnant and had a beautiful cub. I loved my baby so much. We lived together happily in that narrow cage. Even though I was lactating and feeding my cub, they still anesthetized me and poked needles into my flesh to drain me of bile.

When my cub grew a little, they opened the cage and tried to snatch my baby away from me. The horrible pain that was inflicted on me every time they poked me was fresh on my mind. I was so terrified that my cub would have to suffer the same pain. So, hugging her tight, I huddled away in a far corner of my cage.

I was determined to not give my baby away. The keepers poked and prodded me with sticks. But I didn't give in. Then they started to beat me. I still remained calm and unmoving, steadfastly holding my baby to my chest. Then, the keepers got furious and zapped me with an electric charge. I was in excruciating pain but I hugged my baby tight until, finally, I passed out.

I woke up in agony. The keepers thought I was dead and so they were trying to chop off my limbs. For them, preserving my limbs was more important than preserving my life, since they could prepare traditional medicines with them which they could sell for exhorbitant prices. When they chopped one of my forelegs, I let out a terrible cry of pain. They were startled and fled the scene. That's how I escaped into the forest. I don't know if my baby is alive or dead.'

After narrating this sad tale, the bear began sobbing.

'Hek hek.' The yellow monkey sobbed too in sympathy.

'Bow wow.' The dog also began to sob.

Minh didn't draw attention to the silent tears that were coursing down his cheeks. No one could see them in the dark.

When they had all calmed down and dried their tears, Minh began telling them the story about Thu's abduction.

'Well, let me share my story with all of you,' Minh began. 'My sister was kidnapped by bad guys. I have been tracking these guys to save my sister and bring her back home. Please help me find my sister. Anyway, it's late now. We have to get some rest. Tomorrow, we have another long day of trekking.'

'Hek hek. All of you, please go to sleep. I'll be on watch.' The yellow monkey took on this task diligently.

So, bear, dog and Minh hugged each other and fell into a deep slumber.

11

'Bow wow! Wake up! It's already morning!' The dog stroked Minh's face with his paw. Minh turned to hug the bear and continued sleeping. Bear was lying still in Minh's arms. But it pleaded with Tom. 'Let us both sleep for five more minutes.'

Tom, the dog, went downstream to catch fish. Monkey went away in search of guavas to pick, and returned in a while with a lot of guavas but found Minh still fast asleep. The monkey threw a guava at him. Startled, Minh sat up. The monkey clapped his paws and laughed merrily.

Soon, they were all walking along the stream. Bear didn't find walking easy. It couldn't stand upright or walk majestically as is normal. Instead, it walked like a man with a broken leg. So, they couldn't walk fast.

In some places, the trees were so dense that it was impossible to get through them. Here, they had to jump into the stream and wade through the water. One such time, Minh stepped on some smooth round pebbles. He walked very carefully, afraid that he would slip and fall, get hurt and be unable to save his sister. Suddenly, he saw something red floating in the water. He bent down to pick it up. His heart was thumping when he recognized what it was.

'This looks like Thu's slipper,' he exclaimed.

He remembered the slipper that he had found on the first night when he had begun searching for Thu. He quickly undid the bundle that was still slung over his shoulder and took out the slipper to compare. However, he found that the two sandals did not match. They were of different sizes and colours. The truth then suddenly dawned on him: They had not only kidnapped Thu but they had also kidnapped another child along with her.

Once he had worked this out, Minh felt a little less worried. If there were two of them then they would be company for each other and Thu would be less afraid.

They slowly waded upstream. The flow of the river was gentle. Minh suddenly noticed that the water under his feet was no longer clear, and he was perturbed.

'All Stop! Don't move!' Minh's sibilant whisper was steely but hushed.

Everyone understood that Minh was troubled and so they all stopped and turned to him.

'Have you all noticed something rather strange? Look at the stream water. There was no rain recently, yet the water is muddy. This is a sure sign that someone has just gone before us or perhaps even bathed in the stream.'

Minh's friends agreed.

'That's right! You are a keen observer, Minh!'

'I think it's the kidnappers who have "muddied the waters" literally, Minh!'

'Let me shoot ahead to see what's happening', the golden monkey offered and hopping on to a tree, it got lost in the canopy of leaves. Before long, it returned with news.

'False alarm. That was just a buffalo splashing around in the water.'

They all began walking again. The bear seemed to be continually hungry. It would periodically dip its nose into the waters to catch a fish. Tom sniggered at the bear. 'Stop eating so much or soon you'll be as fat as a bear!'

Everyone laughed at Tom's witticism.

Sure enough, in a short while, they came across the buffalo roistering in the stream. Even though it saw them, it didn't stop its rambunctious water sport. They avoided it and carried on wading through the waters.

But the buffalo stopped them with its query, 'Where are you going? Can I join you?'

They halted, not sure where the voice was coming from. Minh turned around to check and realized it was the buffalo, already staggering in their wake. It had only one horn and one eye. Minh declared, 'We are going in search of my sister who has been kidnapped. This is no easy job. So, if you want to join us, be prepared for hard work.'

'I don't mind,' said the buffalo. 'It's so lonely being all alone.'

Minh looked exhausted. He seemed to find it an effort to even place one foot after the other. The monkey piped up: 'Buffalo, my friend, why don't you let Minh ride on your back?'

Minh objected. 'No, I don't want to ride the buffalo'. But it came before Minh and bent its two forelegs in a kneeling position. 'Come on. Get on my back. If you fall ill, who will save your sister?'

Buffalo's words made sense. So, Minh climbed on its back. It ambled slowly with Minh riding it. Everyone trudged along, barely talking to each other. Maybe they were all thinking about the kidnappers, wondering why they were so evil. Did they not have children or siblings? These were children who had been living happily in their own families with their parents, grandparents, and neighbours. But now they had been forcibly wrenched from their homes. Why did they indulge in such cruel deeds? Was it because they didn't love children or because this wasn't theirs? When the children cried, they would probably get angry and hit them. When in their misery and fear they didn't want food, they wouldn't comfort them but instead would let them starve. They would also put the children to work.

All of them jointly resolved to save the poor children.

Minh alighted from the buffalo. He hugged it close to express his gratitude and stroked the buffalo's amputated horn gently. This appeared to really move the buffalo. Minh wiped its tears. Then, he went to the bank of the stream to snip off a sheaf of fresh grass and offered it to the buffalo. It put out its tongue to deftly catch the sheaf and toss it into its mouth. The bear was full. So, he lounged on his back on a slab of rock with his eyes half-closed. Tom, the dog, went downstream to hunt for fish. It caught a long milkfish and brought it back to Minh. Minh stroked Tom, 'You eat it, Tom. I don't eat raw fish. I still have some guavas in my pocket.' He took out a guava and got ready to eat it. He missed rice and noodles so much. It had been four days since he had tasted either rice or vegetables.

The golden monkey had still not returned and everyone was beginning to feel a little impatient and anxious. The longer they waited, the more worried they became.

'Well,' said Minh, 'I think I need to find names for all of you. My name is Minh and the dog is Tom. But do you, buffalo, and bear, have names?

The bear looked shy. 'Bear is my name,' it said coyly.

'No, I mean a name of your own'.

'No, I'm afraid I don't have one,' said the bear.

'Then, I'll name you An.'

'That's a great name. I love it.' said bear.

'What about you, buffalo? Do you have a name?'

'Well, it's buffalo'.

'No, that won't do. I'll name you, Lành. Do you like it?'

'Oh yes. I do', replied the buffalo.

'Ok. Now let's decide on a name for the monkey,' Minh suggested.

'Well, she's very *lém lỉnh* (funny and clever)' An said.

'So, then, let's name her Lém Lỉnh,' Lành said.

'That's an amazing name. Well, from now on we will call the monkey Lém Lỉnh'.

Just then, monkey returned. It came in saying, 'Were you all gossiping about me? From far away, I heard someone mention "golden monkey".'

They all laughed.

'Well, we have given you a new name. From now on, you are no longer just "golden monkey", your name is Lém Lỉnh.'

'I love it. That name suits me.'

'Well, you must already know where the kidnappers are heading. Can you share this with us?'

'Here's what I know. I went a long way ahead but I still didn't set eyes on the kidnappers. But I discovered two small mounds of ash, a little distant from each other. If we keep walking upstream, we'll see this first ash mound. But this ash mound had been extinguished for a while now. I put my palm on it to feel the temperature and it was already cold.' The monkey finished relaying the information.

'Ok. But where's the second ash mound? You've only told us about the first mound,' An enquired.

'Oops. I forgot. I thought I had said everything.' Lém Linh covered its mouth and giggled.

'We should have named you *Hậu Đậu* (clumsy),' Tom scoffed.

'The second ash mound is not near the stream. It is deep inside the forest beside a high mountain. This ash mound too is no longer warm. By the way, Minh, I found a bunch of bananas and brought them back for you.'

'Lém Linh, you are a trooper!' Minh sounded pleased with his monkey friend. 'Lém Linh, can you lead the way, please?'

They all left the stream and cut across the forest path, following in the wake of Lém Linh as they continued walking.

12

This part of the forest path had not been used by anyone. So, it was very dense with giant trees [. . .]

[. . .] So, the beautiful flowers had turned out to be poppies. Now Minh understood why he had never seen them before. His father had been very strict in ensuring that no one in the village grew opium. The schoolteacher had also prohibited anyone from planting poppies. The idea was that if no one grew poppies then there would be no more opium and this would mean no one would get addicted to it. This is why bad people went deep into the forest to cultivate opium plants.

Minh told his friends, 'Poppy is not good. So, let's destroy all these plants.'

Lành felt sad. 'What a pity! These flowers are so pretty.'

An added, 'Actually, poppy isn't all bad. The sap has many medicinal uses. Also, its flowers are beautiful. But unfortunately, humans seem to only want to use it in bad ways. This is why people forbid its cultivation.'

'An, you are very knowledgeable! How do you know all this?' Tom asked.

'I gleaned that information from my keepers who spoke of this while sucking out my bile,' An, the bear, replied.

'If it were "baddies" who planted these poppies, then we must definitely destroy them. I hate bad people,' Lành retorted vehemently. He then bounded up and down the poppy field uprooting all the plants.

Minh stood forlorn, looking around at the Edenic garden that had been trampled underfoot and destroyed by Lành in an instant. Minh's face had paled because this was the first time that the evils of opium had been brought to him first-hand. Previously, he had only heard about it. The dazzling colours of the poppies had exalted his soul and made him happy for a while. Confronted with such beauty, he had wanted to sing, dance and fly. He had wanted to embrace all the flowers and his animal friends, Lành, An, Tom and Lém Lình in his arms. But now he felt heartbroken. Tears rolled down his cheeks. Lém Lình darted to the flowers that had not yet been trampled by Lành and held out pink, white and purple poppies to Minh. They looked so perfect.

'Hek, don't cry, buddy. When you cry, it makes us sad too.'

After having destroyed the opium field, Lành came to kneel beside Minh.

'I'm sorry. But these flowers are really dangerous.'

By now, Minh had overcome his sadness and sat down next to Lành.

'You didn't do anything wrong. What you did was right. It's just that I felt sad watching the beautiful flowers being trampled on.'

Lành paused, then asked softly, 'Do you want to hear my tragic story?'

'Yes. Please, do tell us.' Tom, An, and Lém Lình had all come closer to hear Lành's story.

13

'You all know the age-old idiom in our country—"To get ahead in agriculture, the prime and favoured property is a buffalo". This idiom has been passed down from father to son. We work hard to plow the land and draw the harrow to enable humans to reap a good crop. So, farmers everywhere look after us and care for our welfare. After a lifetime of toil, when we are old and weak, we still offer our flesh and bones to feed humans. We understand that every life form born in this world—from the smallest ant to the huge hippopotamus—has its own specific duties and obligations.'

Lém Linh interrupted, 'Actually, there are germs that are even tinier than ants.'

Tom then interjected, 'Well, there are life forms even smaller than germs.'

An was intrigued, 'Really? What are they?'

'Hmmm . . . I've forgotten,' Tom admitted sheepishly, scratching his ears.

'Do keep quiet, so Lành can continue his story,' Minh appealed, and the buffalo continued.

'Even a blade of grass has its duties and obligations. For example, we buffaloes feed on grass but it can also damage soil and impede paddy cultivation because grass competes for subsistence with the paddy plant. In our universe, humans are the most intelligent life forms. In our eyes, they are imperial beings. So, we want to be useful to them and to serve their needs. We are happy doing this.'

'Thank you, Lành. Being a human myself, it gratifies me to hear you say that', Minh remarked.

'To continue my story, my boss's wife was seriously ill and money was needed for medical treatment. My boss was too poor to support me for long. He sold me. I was glad that I had made some money for him. In my mind, I thought, even if I am slaughtered, I'll gladly go in peace for having served my good master. But what I hadn't bargained for was such cruelty at the hands of humans.

I was bought by the owner of a restaurant specializing in buffalo meat. To demonstrate to customers that they were selling fresh buffalo meat, they tied me to a big tree.

There were many curious onlookers who had gathered around me. Then, they hit me with a sledgehammer. If the human who battered me had been skilled enough, I would have died with just one blow. Perhaps they wanted to demonstrate how a buffalo had been butchered in the Middle Ages! The first blow broke my horn. The second blow, aimed at my ear, hurt badly. The third blow hit me in the eye. I went crazy with pain. Using all my strength, I broke the rope and butted my cruel assailant with my horn. I rushed through the crowded street, ramming against anyone who crossed my path. I made straight for the forest. That's how I landed in the stream. This is my story.'

'That's very sad. Do you hate humans now?' asked Minh.

'I told you before. I only hate bad humans.'

'Lành is right. It's only bad people that we hate,' said An.

'But nowadays, there are a lot of bad people around,' was Tom's rejoinder.

But Lém Linh replied staunchly, 'Our Minh is good.'

'Yeah, I agree,' An acknowledged.

'That's why I followed him,' Lành admitted.

'Thank you all very much, dear friends, and thank you, *Giàng* (God) for your gift of enabling me to understand animal speech. I promise all of you that when I find Thu and return home, I will tell everyone your stories so that they will never be cruel to animals again,' Minh vowed passionately.

They all began trudging through the forest once again. It wasn't long before they came across the second ash mound that Lem Linh had previously discovered. Minh examined the ash mound. It was cool to the touch.

The baddies were very experienced in covering their tracks. They intentionally put out the fire and poured water on it so that no one who came across it would be able to say when the fire had been lit. Minh looked around. He was facing a large mountain. Why hadn't the abductors continued along the stream? How could they get drinking water without the stream? What was there on the other side of the mountain? Was there a village or was it the border? Or was this a false lead to confuse those who might be following behind? But it was getting dark and it would be very difficult to make it across the mountain. So, they had to find a place to bed down for the night.

'We'll stay here for the night since it's getting very dark now. Tomorrow, we will continue our journey,' Minh informed his friends. 'Lém Lỉnh, please go and find ripe bananas. Lành, please look for fresh grass. Tom and An, go find some bamboo rats. I'll sleep for a bit.' Minh leaned back against a huge tree with his bag. His eyes were already heavy with sleep.

14

Lém Lỉnh was shaking Minh awake urgently.

'Wake up! Now! Quick! There's going to be a monsoon downpour! We must run for cover.

Tropical thunderstorms were not novel to Minh. He had witnessed many and was fairly adept at managing to keep safe during heavy rain and flash floods. The previous year, just before the start of the school term, they had had flash floods. From fifth grade onwards, Minh could no longer attend the village school. Instead, he had to go to a school in the town.

This meant that he had to walk nearly five kilometers every day. He had to wake up at the crack of dawn.

He would then walk to the meeting point, to the *cây gạo*, the cotton-tree in the village. There, many village children gathered before walking as a group to the school. The way appeared long and hard when walking alone. But when you walked with a group of friends, it was more fun and your legs didn't protest so much.

Along the way, there was a cave with beautiful stalactites. Previously, when the cave was closed to visitors, people had to climb up to its roof, which took them half-way up the hillock in order to reach the road. But after the cave was cleaned and was opened up as a tourist site by the local government authorities, people could walk through the cave, no longer needing to climb up to its roof.

In summer, when you stepped into the cave, it was as cool as walking into a refrigerator. People came from far and near to visit the caves and to see and touch the beautiful *cây vàng cây bạc* (crotons) that grew there which had attractive, colourful leaves. They also loved to identify the figure of the Buddha and trace shapes of fairies and other folk-characters in the naturally occurring rock-formations that had been contoured by the flowing waters over centuries. They paused to hear the sound of the flowing underground brooks and streams and to seek out 'giant' footprints on the rock. Everyone admired the stalactites that came in different shapes.

The school pupils however—who passed the cave every day on their way to and from the school—did not bother to explore it. They never really looked at the various tourist attractions inside the caves, just hurrying through it to reach their destination as soon as they could. In the mornings they were in a rush to reach school on time and in the evenings, their rumbling tummies made them hurry home.

One year, the flood came without any warning signs. It had been raining continuously for a few days. Minh's father told him that it would be better for him to stay at home rather than walk to school. But Minh didn't want to miss school. His teacher always praised him for being a smart and diligent student. That morning when Minh went to cây gạo, only Lý was there. The two boys walked to school in the rain. As always, they walked through the cave. When both of them had reached the middle, they suddenly heard a loud roar behind them. Then Lý exclaimed in horror,

'Oh my goodness! We are caught in a flash flood.'

They quickly clamoured up a high rock inside the cave. Sitting perched on it, they could hear the sound of the waters as it lashed furiously against the rock. It was pitch dark. They were soon very hungry and cold. They tried to make themselves comfortable in their perch. After their eyes got used to the darkness, they could detect a large slab of rock where they could lie down. They crawled up the stone so afraid that they might slip and fall and get carried away by the furious tide of water into the deep stream. Then they would surely die. They fell asleep at last clinging to each other. After sleeping for a while, they woke up, not knowing if it was day or night. They were so famished that their stomachs seemed to be tied in knots. But after this extreme hunger, they were numb and didn't feel anything. Their mouths became very dry. They stuck out their tongues to lick the raindrops dripping off the rocks. Lý began whimpering. Minh, too, started crying. They both cried in fits and starts.

Suddenly, they heard a voice shouting into the cave. It was accompanied by a flashlight that was swirling round the caves. 'Is anyone there?'

The children were overjoyed. They shouted with all their might:

'We are here.'

The villagers hurried in to save the children and carried them to safety. It turned out that the waters had receded overnight. They had been in the cave for a day and a half. Since the villagers were the local guides for visitors, they knew that the children walked through the cave every day to school. When the flash floods came, it had been around the time when the children walked to school. But they had to wait until the waters receded before they could enter the cave and save the children. They had already cooked rice and kept it ready. So, they took the children to their homes and quickly fed them rice. The children chewed on the rice spiced with shrimp paste in a leisurely manner. After they had eaten they pleaded to go back to their own homes. But one uncle said:

'The stream is still flooded. So, it's not safe for you to go home. Stay with us, we are like your family.'

It was only the following day that both children were finally able to return home. Father and Mother cried so much when they saw Minh until their eyes turned red. They had been terribly worried about Lý and him. But because of the flooded stream, they couldn't go in search of them.

15

The rain had stopped but the sky was still overcast. They all stood around the ash mound. Minh prodded it with a stick and was happy to see that there were still some embers. Because of the rain most of the leaves were wet. So, Minh looked around for some dry leaves to re-light the fire. Then he went to the corn field to pluck some corn cobs. He found some human footprints in the field and his heart started beating fast. He realized that the abductors were not too far away. They were probably still close by. Perhaps, behind that low hill, there might be a house and they were all probably gathered there. Minh realized that he had to be extra watchful and vigilant. If not, he might be kidnapped too. Then imagine the plight of his poor parents! They would be devastated.

Minh returned to the ash mound where his friends were waiting.

'The bad guys are very close. So, we need to spread out, each of us stalking them from a different direction. I'll hide in the cornfield or else these crooks will spot me and kidnap me as well. Lém Linh and Tom, please go, track and find these cruel men first. Then we will discuss how to save Thu.' [. . .]

17[34]

[. . .] Both Lém Linh and Minh stood on the cliff top looking down at the house where they knew Thu was kept by her jailers.

Lém Linh began, 'Do you realize that that one-storey timber building with loopholes is actually used as a

---

[34] In chapters, 15, 16, Minh and his animal friends discovered where the traffickers are keeping the children. Realizing a boy was being taken to be executed, Minh and his friends wanted to save Thu as quickly as possible.

blockhouse. It is like a fort with just one door. There are men there guarding Thu. I'm positive she's there. When I came to scout around, I found that there were two men guarding the door.'

Minh agreed. 'The other two men, their mates, were the ones we just saw,' he said. 'They were tucking into a lot of rice wine. I'm sure by now they are fast asleep in a drunken stupor in the forest. We need to hurry now. I have a plan. I want you to distract those two guards so that they leave the door and follow you. Then I can sneak inside the house.'

'What do you think I should do?'

'Go get some ripe guavas, bananas, or figs. Then approach the door. Sit down calmly in front of these guys and start eating. I know these guys will want to catch you. Monkeys are caught and sold for high prices.'

Lém Linh turned pale. 'I know. If they have a gun and they *dòm* me, I'm sure to die.'

Minh was puzzled. "Đòm" you? What does that mean?'

'Don't you know?'

'No. Please explain.'

'That is slang for shoot.'

'You seem to know a lot of slang words. You must tutor me in them sometime.' Minh sounded envious. 'But for now, let's focus on saving Thu. Lém Linh, you are very quick. So, don't be afraid. Just pretend to be a stupid monkey hanging around and eating wild fruits. When they come near you, just dart away. In this way, drag them farther and farther away from the house. Then I can sneak in.' Minh's words galvanized Lém Linh.

'All right. I'll do my best.'

'Dear friend, you are amazing. I promise to never part from you'.

Saying so, Minh followed in the wake of Lém Linh. Secretly, he was very worried about his friend. He plotted to find a way to save him. He gathered egg-sized stones and pocketed them. If the baddies attempted to shoot Lém Linh, he would hit them on the head with the stones.

Lém Linh followed Minh's instructions to the letter. Exactly as Minh had predicted, the two guards fell for his trick. They goaded each other to pursue and catch the monkey. 'Why don't you block this side and I'll block the other so it can't escape. We need to lure this monkey into our bunker. The money from monkey-mucilage is even more than what we can make from kids.'

True to their plan, Lém Linh gradually enticed the guys out into the open, away from the door. Minh was able to sneak in. In the dark house, Minh called out softly, 'Thu, are you there?' [. . .]

[. . .] 'Hush, quiet'. Minh silenced them. 'Both of you wait for me. I can't save you now because the bad guys outnumber us. But be patient and wait for me. Don't be afraid. Make sure that you don't let on about me to the baddies.'

'Ok. But please come back quickly. I'm terrified,' Thu whimpered.

'Don't cry, Thu. I'll save you. We have been following your tracks for several days now. I am confident of being able to save you.'

Minh hid behind the door trying to slip out without being spotted. The two guards were still busy chasing after

Lém Linh. Minh ran out, climbed up the hill and then hailed Lém Linh with a howl. Hearing the signal, Lém Linh hopped on to the branch of a tree and disappeared from the sight of four merciless, greedy eyes which searched in vain.

Minh and Lém Linh lost no time in going in search of An and Lành. They had discovered a pond in the valley. Lành was bathing in the water and thoroughly enjoying himself. An, meanwhile, had been busy catching a lot of fish to bring ashore.

Minh called out to them to gather around him. But Tom was missing. Minh called out, 'Tom, where are you?' He had to call out repeatedly before he heard Tom's voice.

'I'm terrified. Really scared.'

Minh was stumped. 'What is scaring you?'

'I smell gunpowder.'

'From where?'

'Over there.' Tom came into sight, pointing to the range of hills facing them.

'Then, all the more reason for us to hurry,' Minh rapped out urgently. 'We've got to be really quick. They might have called for more reinforcements. Or, perhaps, the organ traders are already here.'

Minh quickly recounted his meeting with Thu and Thảo. He pleaded, 'Quick, how can we rescue them?'

They all scratched their foreheads trying to think up plans for rescue.

Lành said, 'I'm going to butt them'.

An added, 'I'll hit them hard'.

Tom declared, 'I'll bite them.'

Lém Linh came in with 'I'll put out their hair from their scalp'.

Minh shouted out enthusiastically, 'I've got it figured. I'll go find a rope to tie them up. Meanwhile, An, you should attack one of them. Throw him to the ground and then grasp him in a real "bear hug" while I tie him up. Lành and Tom, both of you have to attack the other guy. Hold on to him until I can tie him up as well. Right now, it's just two of them. So, we need to do this quickly before the others arrive.'

Minh quickly gathered some strong vines and they all trooped silently in to the house. An led the way, followed by Lành. Then Tom followed with Lém Lỉnh behind. Minh was at the end of the line. Minh hid himself behind a bush waiting for the right moment to jump out and act.

An staggered out into the open and approached one of the two men, who was seated. The other saw the bear loping towards his companion and jumped up to escape to the forest. He heard his companion's terrified scream and glanced back to find that he had keeled over in shock and was lying prostrate on the ground. He turned to flee but was accosted by a one-eyed buffalo with a broken horn and a snout-less dog, both ready to attack him. This man too stood frozen stiff with fear. Minh couldn't help thinking, 'Hey, I believed you guys were the very devil but turns out you are just cowards.' He rushed out of the bushes, tied them both up one after the other. He then cautioned his friends to be alert and rushed into the house.

'Thu, Thảo, I'm here to rescue you. Hurry up!'

They replied in chorus, 'We're here, we're tied up and can't stand up.'

Minh ran out and rummaged through the pockets of the bad guys searching for a lighter. Watching them from the hills earlier, he had seen one of them smoking. Sure enough, he found it. Minh lit it to search for the children in the dark. He found the bound-up children and rushed to them. Minh quickly untied them. Thu clung to her brother's neck, sobbing. Minh hugged her tight and cried out loud in joy. Lém Lỉnh let the two of them cry a little before pulling at Minh's hand and urging him out.

'Hek, hek. Come, let's go. The others will soon be here.'

'Hek, hek. You're right, Lém Lỉnh. Thu, Thảo, can you both walk?' Minh's words were rushed.

'Oh yes, we can,' they replied instantly.

'Ok. let's go then.'

Minh and his four-legged friends felt extremely happy. He kept on thanking his friends numerous times. They all chuckled. An held Minh's shoulders and said, 'There's no need to thank me anymore. Instead, later, when you grow up, you can open a shelter for abused animals like us.'

'For sure!' Minh replied. 'I might even open an animal rescue park. These hills are vast with plenty of space. We can open a huge rescue center here.'

They all walked out into the forest chatting. 'Maybe it will be the first animal shelter in Vietnam,' Lém Lỉnh said, smiling happily at the thought.

Translated from 'Minh Lém Lỉnh, trâu một sừng, gấu cụt tay và chó mất mõm' in *Văn nghệ quân đội* (online) January 4, 2024.

'Garden' by Nguyễn Nhật Linh

Rose Villa (2022)

Hoàng Tố Mai (1972)

When Lam was twelve, his family and he moved to the Old Quarter. Before that, his mother and brothers had lived in the suburbs right at the far end of a long, dark, quiet lane. Lam didn't remember his father, who had been a geologist and hence had had to travel frequently. After setting off to survey a site in a mountainous region, his father had not returned. His body was never recovered and people wondered if he had fallen into some deep abyss. Lam, however, refused to believe what the people said. He often told his younger brother, 'I have a feeling that Dad is lost and wandering around in a different dimension. In all probability, he will return one day. It might be in a few years or it might even be after hundred years'. When mother heard him, she would smile rather sadly and think, *How carefree childhood is! I wish I could enjoy just one day of such happiness.* Later, recollecting those days, Lam also realized that their days in the suburban neighbourhood had been so tranquil.

Houses there were surrounded by walls covered in lush, beautiful creepers and plants including Tonkinese, passion fruit, Chinese hibiscus, silverberry, and mulberry, alongside bougainvillea, honeysuckle, Cananga tree, and so on. I recall that children often used to play at stealing the flowers and fruits from each others' gardens. The silverberries that grew abundantly in the house adjacent to Lam's were never left long enough to ripen. Whenever they turned a little yellow, children climbed on top of each other to form a human pyramid and picked all the berries. When he recalled those days, it was like recalling festive days; they were as full of excitement [. . .]

[. . .] The only house in the entire neighbourhood that was beyond their ken was one that was fenced by high, old, laterite walls liberally covered by dog-roses. These roses mysteriously bloomed all year round. The flowers hung down the walls in an enchantingly alluring way. The children found it a great pity that the walls were too high to scale. So, they were unable to reach the flowers.

For the children in the neighbourhood, this was a magical villa completely shrouded in mystery, which is why the villa was seen as being special. The fragrance of the dog-rose blooms was similar to those of the pink rose but somehow it felt more soothing. The difference was so subtle that those who rushed past in a hurry or whose minds were preoccupied would not have picked it up. Even among the children, only Lam and some of the girls took deep breaths when they played around the walls that surrounded the house. No one had ever seen the owner's face clearly. The wooden gate was always tightly closed.

Occasionally, the owner would open the gate a tiny bit to pay the electricity bill or some such thing but then would immediately close it shut again.

One day, Lam, spying a bamboo ladder that had been left outside by an absent-minded builder, stacked it against the wall hoping to pick up some of the shoots of the dog-rose plant for the girls. The ladder was high enough for Lam to shimmy up the wall and peek inside. Up there, Lam was accosted by a pleasant aromatic breeze. He saw a big garden. The house was located at its center and was shrouded by broad leaves. Most of the trees appeared mature with strong branches that stretched long and wide. In the front yard, there were many carefully manicured flower bushes.

As he was absorbing the beautiful garden in bemused wonder, Lam was startled to suddenly hear a cry of pain emanating from the garden below. 'Goodness! It hurts so much!' said the voice. The words were followed by a shrill shriek that appeared to be coming from beneath a bunch of hanging white roses. Looking down, Lam saw a girl of around ten waving her arm wildly all the while complaining about the pain and muttering, 'What type of thorn is it that it stings so badly?' As she complained, the girl happened to raise her eyes and she caught sight of Lam. The terrified boy tried to climb down but the girl began waving her arms excitedly. 'Please come into the garden', she beckoned. 'It is easy. You can step down on the horse's head'. Peering down, Lam saw a big statue of a horse. A short while later, he had landed in the garden.

Holding his hand excitedly, the little girl rushed into the house even as a call emerged from within. '*Hương An* (fragrance of peace), please don't go out. Stay inside. It's quite windy out there.'

'I'm coming,' the girl responded in a silken voice. *So her name is An*, thought Lam. An looked at him and said in an eager voice, 'I know you. You are Lam. Sometimes I would climb up the horse's head and watch you pluck silverberries for a group of children. Aren't I right?'

Lam reluctantly nodded his head. He wondered why he had never seen Hương An before though they both lived in the same neighbourhood. *She is graceful but rather exotic*, Lam thought. She wore a loose, long-sleeved blouse with prints of yellow and green flowers. She looked rather delicate in that thin blouse. Whenever a breeze blew by, the blouse fluttered—almost as though it would drift off her and fly away.

Though the girl was holding on to his hands, Lam still felt uncertain and ashamed to have walked into a stranger's house without proper permission. If his mother came to know about it, he was sure she would punish him for this misdemeanour. Approaching a room on the left side of the house, An opened the door and led Lam inside. The room housed several volumes of books. It looked like a library. The shelves, chairs, and tables made of sindora wood were inlaid with exquisite woodwork and appeared antique. This kind of furniture only existed in pagodas of contemporary times.

'Do you study here?' Lam asked An.

'Yes. I also read stories. My mother has told me that long ago this was said to be the "reading room" of my maternal grandparents.' she replied.

Lam nodded, 'Oh so, this is a library.' Lam noticed that the room was large. But all the things there were arranged tastefully but modestly. The beautiful centrepiece was a huge vase filled with exquisite dog-rose blossoms that brightened the whole room. Seeing Lam glance in a rather dazzled way at the flower vase, An giggled.

'Every day, I make the excuse of collecting flowers for the vase to run to the garden and climb up the horse's statue to peer out,' she explained. The subtle aroma of the rose blossoms soothed some of Lam's anxieties and he ventured to ask her, 'How long have you stayed here? Why haven't I seen you before?'

She answered readily enough, 'I have always stayed here. But I'm not allowed to leave my compound and I don't particularly want to because every time I do, I get very sick.'

Lam peered out through the window. A magical scene unfolded before his eyes. Beside the cool blue pond, a flamboyance of flamingos had gathered. They stood on small rocks overgrown with moss. Some were pecking at their feathers while others were flapping around. Some even opened their wings wide as though they were engaging in a complex dance routine. On the opposite side of the pool was a large tiger who appeared to be sunbathing. The tiger gazed indifferently at Lam. Like a large, lazy cat, it yawned with its mouth wide open. Then, it laid down its head and slumbered with half-closed eyes. 'What a true gentleman,' he heard An say, and he turned around to see who she was talking about. But there was no one else there. 'I meant the tiger,' she explained.

That was the first time Lam had ever encountered a tiger without a fence in-between and that lack of barrier was deeply satisfying. He wanted to rush out and gently touch its fabled black striped fur mixed with brilliant gold. 'My goodness! Your house is like a zoo,' said Lam to

An, staring at her in surprise. But it seemed that she had never visited a zoo and didn't quite know what it was.

'That's a place where animals are kept captive and people can buy tickets to watch them from behind fences.'

'Oh, I've heard about this place from my mum but I think watching imprisoned animals must be so boring. It makes no sense to do that,' An responded. 'If you come here in the afternoons,' she continued, 'you will see many kinds of birds gathering around the pond and chirping with joy. When I approach the pond, they swoop down, flying over my head.'

'Really?' Lam was amazed.

'Yes. Sometimes a white eagle descends to perch on my arm. I usually look for bugs in the garden to feed them. Because of that, I've been pricked by thorns many times.' [...]

[...] After meeting An, Lam would catch himself constantly looking at the rose tree where he had once leaned a ladder and climbed into a strange house. Lam longed to climb up into the house again but didn't dare. He wished Hương An would peek out so he could glimpse at her. Suddenly, on Saturday, Lam saw a tiny hand waving to him and he spied An's alert black eyes shining behind the green foliage. The constructor's ladder still lay on the ground. Lam deftly lifted it, leaned it against the dog-rose tree, and climbed inside, swift as lightning. That day, An was wearing a lovely white skirt the colour of fresh rice. She wore a wide green hat—the colour of leaves—on her head.

When she ran around in the lush garden or hid herself behind bushes, her skinny form seemed to merge with the foliage and disappear. Like the last time time, An took Lam to the library. Glancing outside, Lam found the 'gentleman' lazing fairly close by. On taking a closer look, Lam felt that he looked longer and wider than before. His glittering eyes seemed to look directly at Lam, who was starting to feel terrified.

An appeared extremely amused. 'Do not worry. Just stay in this room. Don't enter other rooms. Then he will roar and chase you,' she instructed.

'Does your mum know that you've invited me here? enquired Lam.

'Well, I can't quite remember,' replied An. 'Last week, mum was very busy with her chores. She's always working. Perhaps I didn't have time to request her permission. But there won't be any problem.'

Lam was still anxious. 'If your mum isn't happy with my visits, I wouldn't dare step into the house. But that's no big deal. We can still meet in school during the day,' Lam ventured.

'I don't go to school. I just study at home with my mum.' An said.

'But why?'

'Since I was little, whenever I ventured out, I fell ill. So my mother insisted I stay inside the house'.

Lam wanted to find out where her father was but felt awkward because she had never mentioned him. It was likely that the father didn't stay with them.

Then, An gave Lam the same volume of fairy tales as the previous time. She wanted him to read out the *Trương Chi* story to her. 'Please read this for me,' she pleaded. 'But you can read it yourself, can't you?' Lam queried. 'Of course, but listening to someone else read is far more fun. If one person reads, it informs two people', she retorted. Lam burst out laughing, lifted the book, and read with as much expression as he could infuse into the words for An. This tale though sounded rather strange. Lam hadn't heard of this story before. Lam couldn't understand why such a regal maiden, daughter of a royal prime minister could have fallen so passionately in love with the singing voice of a poor boatman. The princess was determined to see him in person. However, when she did see him, she found him ugly. So she decided to stay away from him and thus rejected him. But the tale had a haunting ending. Trương Chi was so overcome with his passion for the lady that he gradually languished away and finally died. After many years, though his body had turned to dust, his heart continued to beat and over time condensed into a jade stone. Later, the precious stone was carved into a cup and offered to the prime minister. One day, when the young daughter poured water into this jade cup, she saw an image of a young man ferrying a boat gradually appear on the cup. The image was accompanied by a beautiful song filled with sadness and sorrow. The lady cried and her tears fell into the cup which dissolved into water. Lam felt that this was not like a typical fairy tale. There was no 'happy ever after'. Instead, there was a lingering sense of desolation. However, Hương An seemed more interested in the details of the jade cup.

'I want to have a cup like that but where will I find it? I want to look at that cup and imagine what I want,' she said.

Lam remarked 'Reality is still better and of greater value.'

Ann said, 'I won't cry when I look at the cup or else it might dissolve.'

Lam was amused and wondered at her innocence. Looking around the library, he saw an old cassette in a corner. *It probably doesn't work*, he thought. He asked An, 'Don't you have a television or a computer?'

'What are they?' she enquired.

Lam gradually came to realize the extent of the girl's isolation from the outside world and all of its gadgets. After listening to Lam's description of a television, she recalled that she had indeed had one earlier. 'My eyes hurt so much looking at the screen that my mum gave it away', she explained. Lam realized that he couldn't bring Hương An his exciting comic books. She wouldn't be able to understand half the things that were commonplace in the outside world such as a flashlight, a smartphone, a laptop . . . the list was endless.

While he had been absorbed in his thoughts, Hương An had fetched a tray of some light green food for him. 'Here is some rice flake pudding and ice cream. Please taste them,' she entreated.

'Did you make these all by yourself?'

'No. I didn't. I just helped mum.'

The tray and the bowls were made of porcelain encrusted with jade. On the outside of the pudding bowl there were some ancient hieroglyphs that were not very clear. The ice-cream bowl was smaller. It contained an ink brush painting of a tiny boat floating alone on a calm river. Lam pointed this out to An and remarked, 'You see, this bowl only lacks the grievous voice of Trương Chi.' An was very excited. 'Tonight, I'll burn a candle and pour water into the bowl. If I hear a song, I'll note down the lyrics and memorize them,' she said solemnly.

Though Lam wanted to tease An, he pretended to agree with her and nodded.

That afternoon was delightful. The rice-flake ice cream and the pudding were so delicious that they induced in Lam a feeling of well-being and comfort. As he was luxuriating dreamily in their taste and savouring the feeling, he was jerked to reality when he heard his mother's call. He hurriedly climbed up to the horse's head to jump out and quickly checked with An, 'When will I see you again?' An seemed to remember something all of sudden. Quickly waving her hands, she said, 'Today my name is not Hương An. Every Thursday, please remember to call me *Tiểu Lụa* (Little Silk Piece).' Lam was perplexed. 'Why?' he asked. 'You are still you. Why should your name change?' 'Well, today, my name is Tiểu Lụa.'

'What a strange name, how did you get it?' Lam wondered. 'I made it up myself,' she replied, smiling. 'On Fridays and Saturdays, I study with my mum. So please come here on Sunday at noon.'

'Sure! Bye-bye!' said Lam.

As planned, promptly on Sunday at noon, Lam climbed up the ladder. He saw that An was waiting for him by the horse's statue. She wore brown silk trousers and a pink blouse with her neckline shaped like a lotus leaf, embroidered with images of colourful tiny fruits.

'Have you been waiting long for me? queried Lam.

'For a while, yes'.

A fresh wind blew in making the world within the compound different to the one outside, which was filled with heat and damp. Lam slowly but surely made his way to the library. The 'gentleman' was lying lazily at the entrance. He looked Lam straight in the eye with his penetrating gaze. Lam felt scared. He had to come to terms with the fact that this was no mere, large, cat but definitely a powerful tiger. Suddenly, it came to life with a wild gesture that terrified Lam. The 'gentleman' jumped up growling. Lam felt as though there was an earthquake. He felt the whole garden tremble. The birds twittered, flying away fast. The flamingos flapped their wings in panic. Lam felt as though he was lost in a wild place.

Once inside, Lam spotted a delicate Chinese lacquer box inlaid with mother of pearl. The box looked very old and its colour had mellowed over time. Lam had seen this box on a previous visit. It had then been placed in the bookshelf along with the rest of the books. Lam wondered why An had brought it out now. As though reading his thoughts, An gently told him, 'Today is a sunny day and I want to expose these objects to the sunlight'. She opened the box and an array of colours emanated from it, each one vying with its companion for a chance to dazzle under the light that was shining through the window.

'This is the jade box that my maternal grandmother left,' An informed Lam, who gaped at the splendorous display of gems of various shapes and colours studded in necklaces, rings and chains.

Even to Lam's ignorant eyes, the jade looked very valuable like imperial green jadeite. Since they were all ancient, they no longer had a bright green look but had a softer hue which still looked beautiful.

An said, 'My mum said that old jade is more valuable than fresh jade. But I prefer fresh jade.'

'Really? I prefer old jade.' Lam remarked.

'Ha ha! You are like my mum. She too prefers old jade. Now look at these bright, very attractive red stones.

They are rubies,' An explained. Interlaced with the jade stones, Lam noticed, were gold coins of different sizes. These were imprinted with the national emblems of ancient dynasties.

'Oh my god!' Lam exclaimed, shocked, 'was anyone in your family a pirate?'

'How would I know?' she laughed.

'I have heard that my maternal grandfather used to sail the oceans. He would have been the only one who could have enlightened us on whether he later became a pirate or not.'

An then carried the box carefully into the garden placing it on the lawn outside, where the sunlight was even brighter. Lam offered to help her but she declined saying, 'The "gentleman" will not permit it. He will roar angrily if you touch it.'

Only then did Lam understand why the 'gentleman' had been lying right at the entrance of the library as though to prevent his entry. He had probably known that his little mistress had brought out the family treasures.

Lam asked An curiously, 'But why do you need to expose these treasures to sunlight?'

'In order for them to drink in the sun and to brighten up their fading colours.'

'Did someone ask you to do this?'

'No. I thought of it myself. My mum frequently dries ginseng in the sun to make it last longer. I too bask in the sunlight each morning to avoid getting rickets. It's always good to get exposed to sunlight, I think. It increases your energy levels.'.

The 'gentleman', Lam noticed, closely followed An as she carried the treasures out of the library. When she placed the box down on the lawn, the tiger immediately lay down nearby with half-closed eyes. Back in the room, Lam recalled that he had to get back home by 1.00 p.m. to babysit his little brother so his mother could leave for work. He asked An urgently, 'Do you have a clock or a watch? I need to get home by 1.00 p.m. today'.

'We don't need a clock. As soon as the Chinese Hwamei birds begin singing, we'll know that it's time for you to head home,' An reassured Lam. 'Now, I'm going to go and fetch some fruit,' she said as she disappeared. She returned with two dark trays that were made of rare aromatic wood. One contained fresh fruits while the other was covered. The young girl placed both trays on the table with something approaching excitement and announced, 'Today, we are going to play an interesting quiz game. In the covered tray are dried fruits while the open tray has fresh fruits of the same kind. Now you have to close your eyes. I will let you taste the dried fruits one by one. As you taste them, if you can identify them accurately, you have the right to a gold coin.'

'And what if I fail to identify them?' Lam enquired.

'Then you have to make do with the coins that I will select for you,' An said.

Lam laughed. 'Well, that's not too bad a deal at all. Whatever I answer, I will still get a prize, after all!

Just for fun, Lam shut his eyes and named more than ten dried fruits. But it wasn't easy because each of them smelled very different from their fresh counter-parts. This was especially true of the lychee and longan. Though Lam tasted these two dried fruits several times, he still failed to recognize their smells, and eventually, gave up.

Hương An burst into a clear, bell-like laughter. 'It's a deal,' she said, "if you lose you *have* to take the coin chosen by me.'

'No. I don't need them. Also, did you check with your mother? Have you got her permission?' Lam asked.

'Oh, she can't be bothered.' But Lam was troubled. 'I think she does care. Also, even if she permits it, I won't take any coin from you.' As they conversed, Hương An seemed to consume a lot of fruit. She seemed to love eating fruits. Now, she asked him, 'Among all the exquisite things you saw in the old box, which one did you like best?' 'Well . . . I liked the imperial green jadeite and the gold coins,' Lam answered hesitantly. 'I thought the same,' she said. 'This is why I thought I'd give you the coin as a reward for the game. I like them because they are similar to the ones in the story, "Hidden Gold in an Island".'

'Yes, I too have that book.' Lam declared eagerly. 'I have the comic book version. The pictures of the pirate's gold treasure look wonderful.

'Are the pictures better than the ones in the jade box?' she enquired.

'No, of course not!' But the treasures pictured there looked so large that one might need a truck to carry all of them.'

An smiled with enthusiasm. 'Please, can you lend me your comic book?

'Yes, of course. You can keep it for yourself.' Lam replied.

The two chatted together amicably, their conversation interspersed with a lot of laughter until they heard the bewitching sound of the Chinese Hwamei.

Lam reluctantly left the library and got ready to go back home. 'Goodbye, Hương An . . . Oh, sorry! I should say, goodbye, Tiểu Lụa!' Lam said, smiling cheekily.

'No, no,' An countered, 'today, my name is not Tiểu Lụa.'

'Oh! Then, who are you today?'

'I am *Hải Nương* (Ocean Princess),' she retorted and Lam burst out laughing. He wondered a little at how he managed to remember the names she called herself on different days. 'Alright! Goodbye Hải Nương,' Lam said, even as he pondered over what her name would be when next he saw her.

Only when Lam arrived home did he realize that he had forgotten to fix a time for their next meeting. He decided that he would stand near the stone horse every day at noon until Hương An appeared. However, that wish was thwarted because his mum informed him of a sudden decision during dinner. 'We are moving out of this neighbourhood,' she announced. It transpired that she had bought a seafood stall in *Đồng Xuân* market for a reasonable price from her oldest brother. So, the whole family would have to move to the Old Quarter to take up the new business. Their house in the suburb too was to be sold off quickly to a neighbour since his son was getting married and would need to set up a new home. Since the house in the Old Quarter was sold by the uncle, they had the liberty of moving in quickly—in just ten days.

In the new house, though his mother was bringing in more money, Lam felt stifled and constrained. It took him some time but gradually, he got reconciled to city life. Occasionally, when people from his old neighbourhood visited, they even complimented him on his new 'city look'.

Ten years passed by quickly. Lam graduated but couldn't find a job. So, he helped his mother out in the seafood stall. But some months later, news leaked out about how the Formosa

Steel manufacturers were illegally discharging their toxic waste into the open waters. They were polluting hundreds of kilometres of coastal waters off Central Vietnam. Viewing news on the internet of the death of thousands of fish that were living deep in the sea, their carcasses floating up to form a dense, white layer along the coast, Lam realized that the seafood business would be in big trouble. Everywhere, seafood businesses collapsed because customers were afraid to eat fish from the polluted waters. Lam's family sold their remaining fish for next to nothing and finally, were forced to sell their stall. His family didn't have any income. As a last, desperate resort, his mother opened up her ledger to go through the list of customers carefully to see if any of her regular customers owed her money for their purchases. A few days later, his mother ordered Lam to return to the old neighbourhood to ask their old neighbour, who had in fact bought their old house, to repay the debt for purchasing seven kilograms of crawfish.

Lam saw that his old neighbourhood in the suburbs had changed radically. Now the houses stood lined up so tightly next to each other with barely an inch to spare that it was difficult to identify his former house. The spread of Tonkinese creepers wasn't there any longer. The owner had fenced in the front year to make it a garage to park his vehicles. It looked stuffy and dismal. Before he rang the bell, he could hear the husband yelling at his wife. But after the bell rang, only their child peeped out, looked at him, asked if it was indeed Lam, and then disappeared. The argument seemed to have stopped abruptly. Then, the little boy peered out again and said, 'My parents aren't at home. They'll only return in a few days.'

Lam shook his head wearily. Given the current economic situation, it would be a fortunate lender who could collect his debt. As Lam was about to walk back home disappointed at the outcome, he sensed a strange yet familiar fragrance engulfing him. Of course! It was the sweet scent of the dog-rose. He thought how strange it was that it bloomed so vividly in the middle of this freezing December. As he walked close to the quiet house with a tall, imposing gate, Lam heard a lilting voice within.

After he reached home, Lam held on to the box tightly as he climbed to the upper floor. Lam's brother was sleeping. He looked better. Lam went to the terrace, sat down on a chair, and placed the box on his thighs. The terrace was usually deserted. Lam loved this retreat, where in isolation he enjoyed the orchid cacti blooming at night. When he was there, he often remembered the villa with the exquisite garden and the dog-rose. Sometimes, in the midst of his noisy life beset by a multitude of cares, he wondered if he had dreamed up the villa. That patch of heaven appeared so far removed from his hum-drum life.

But now, Lam had the box in front of him, the only tangible object he had left from the secret villa. There it was, cool, silky, and solid in his hands. Lam opened it cautiously and was dazzled by the arrangement inside. An had laid out various fruits and pieces of jelly to resemble exquisite pieces of jewelry. Fresh green grapes were arranged to look like an authentic jade necklace; a heart-shaped ruby pendant was formed with pomegranate seeds; tender lotus seeds were strung to resemble a pearl bracelet; wild apple juice was congealed to resemble an amber leaf; the tender coconut flesh was fashioned into a white onyx and a grape jelly became an amethyst flower; Beneath these fruits he found a cake made of chocolate gold coins. He picked up a coin and placed it in his mouth. This delectable cake must be a gourmet product of some expensive European chocolatier, he thought, as it dissolved in his mouth leaving behind the taste of expensive cocoa. Lam picked up another coin. But this was cold and heavy. It slipped through his fingers and fell to the floor with a heavy clang. Lam realized in a moment of panic that it was truly made of gold and was carved with the national emblem of some eighteenth-century European nation. The coin had been hidden inside the jade box.

In a moment of sheer exhilaration, Lam realized that it was Hương An that he had seen that day. Her old habits had not changed in the past ten years. She still played the game of changing her name every day. She had named herself Lam An, which was a sign that she hadn't forgotten him. Lam recalled the basket of vegetables and roots that he had seen beside the 'gentleman' tiger. That must have been the jade box. Evidently, she still continued with the habit of exposing the jade box to sunlight whenever she could. So, she hadn't traveled far at all. She was very much there in that house with the gentle breeze and the warm sunlight, in peace and serenity, passing her time by occasionally making sweets in exquisite flavours. She had generously bequeathed Lam with a valuable family heirloom.

She was wholesome and sustaining while Lam existed at the margins of this reality. It was as though there were two separate worlds divided by a mere dog-rose fence. She always remained on the other side of it insulated from all that was evil and dirty in the wretched, crowded, noisy world outside, where unexpected dangers lurked in behind every corner. Beyond the dog-rose fence, she inhabited a perfect world, which appeared dreamlike.

Lam slowly straightened up. As he continued gazing at the exquisite figures in the box, images from the past rushed in. Slam! His mother had pushed the door so hard that the loud sound jolted him from his reverie. He heard snatches of the exchange between his mother and brother.

'Where is Lam? How are you feeling now? Yes . . . you look better.'

'Sorry, what did you ask? Oh, the debt-collection? Well, I managed to get half of it at least. I will need to go back several more times before I can wrest the remaining amount from the debtors.'

Lam wiped his tears and hastily shutting the box, he hid it behind the white rose plant. He slowly returned to the kitchen and started helping his mother replace the bulb so that she could cook dinner on time. He would have to tell his mother about his unsuccessful attempt at debt collection from their former neighbours. But he wouldn't mention anything about the dog-rose villa. There are some stories that need to be kept secret forever. Only when you feel that you can no longer hold them within you, only then should you divulge them by writing them down, late at night, by the gradually unfolding petals of the orchid-cactus.

Translated from 'Biệt thự tầm xuân'
Nhà văn và cuộc sống, số 9 năm 2022, pp. 41–53.

Raw Fish (2005)

Nguyễn Ngọc Thuần (1972-)

It was already far too late . . . too late to change Uncle's habits. His eating habits, if studied by fish, should have taught them life lessons about survival. He ate fish day and night. His toothache—which meant he was constantly in a state of pain—did not prevent him from gobbling up large quantities of delicious fish; even as his teeth hurt when he chewed on them. There were several instances when I caught him trying to pull out his teeth. If he could have managed it, he would have done so a long time ago.

My father had his theory on this—'It is important to know how to endure pain,' he would say. However, he wasn't at all pleased with my Uncle's indiscriminate eating habits. In a strange way, it seemed to cause my father an incomprehensible sense of sadness. Nevertheless, he still went fishing every day to procure fish for Uncle. He would dive into the lake wearing only a pair of shorts, which he would fold around to trap the fish. Father was an experienced fisherman. At times, when he stepped ashore, he was heavy with fish because you could see that his shorts were full of them. My Uncle would stand at the shore, admiring him from afar. Despite a lifetime of devouring fish, he personally had never caught one. He was only good at eating them. When he opened his mouth, it was full of decayed teeth. It wasn't only the fish who would have been afraid of his mouth. Most humans would have been too.

My father rationed the fish he gave my uncle. It was just one fish a day. But that was more recently. Earlier, in the past, my father would catch a school of thirty fish and release them into the beautiful fish-tank, more an aquarium than a tank, at their home. He calculated that this would mean that he could go back to work in peace for a whole month. But father's calculations didn't pan out since my Uncle would polish off the entire colony of fish in just twelve days. Some days he would eat up to five fish. Eating so many raw fish would invariably upset his stomach and he would throw up greenish-yellowish bile, which was absolutely disgusting. By noon, the whole house would stink to high heaven. All the neighbourhood cats and dogs would sniff the air and go wild. Uncle would just stand looking at the dead fish that he had thrown up. He felt betrayed that he had to give up his flavoursome meal to cats and dogs. But, of course, he couldn't eat them again, either. This was the tragedy of his life. He would always regret the fact that he had not limited himself to only four fish because then he may have retained his delicious meal. But the following morning, the whole ritual would begin again. He simply could not resist overeating since he always felt so hungry and greedy when he saw all that delectable fish.

After this period of trial and error, when my Uncle regularly ingested and ejected five fish a day, my father no longer trusted him to curtail his greed despite Uncle fervently promising that he would never eat too many. Father made sure that he kept him supplied with just one fish a day in the morning just before he went to work in the field. He would drop this fish gently and courteously into the fish-tank, where there were statues of two folk gods playing chess, as though he suspected that they were silently witnessing his act. Just as other people would bring their children a bowl of *phở* and place it on the table for breakfast, he supplied his brother with just one fish for his breakfast. Thus it was that this big tank, nearly half-a square metre, had just one fish swimming in it. This made Uncle rather sad. Moreover, when he had eaten that sole fish, the tank looked even more desolate and empty. He hated looking at this empty aquarium for it made it only look larger and wider. This meant that he didn't eat his fish in a hurry. He took delight in watching it swim, nodding his head in a satisfied way. He would resist until early afternoon when his screaming innards would make him give in to temptation. He would then tragically mutter, 'goodbye fish' and stepping close and reaching into the tank, he would pick up the ill-fated fish to eat it. Although the fish would struggle madly between his fingers, he would eat it delicately, biting its head off lightly. He ate efficiently and with great satisfaction. When morning had passed, my father would return from the fields and in his conical cape held upside down, he would hold a new fish which was to be Uncle's breakfast the following day.

Uncle would look at the fish in the cape and demand sulkily, 'Why is it so small?'

'Bigger breeds are not available. The season is over. If you don't like it, why don't you go out and try fishing yourself?' My father's retort would be abrupt.

Even as Uncle watched, the fish would disappear. My father would have secreted the fish away so that my Uncle would never be able to find it. My father habitually hid it in a secret place that my Uncle could never discover. He would only discover the fish the following morning. This secret place was actually under my father's bed. Here, there were no statues of folk gods playing chess. There was no enchanting bridge. But this tank was home to a natural world that was in every way more splendorous than Uncle's aquarium because it contained its most essential feature, the fish. In fact, there were dozens of fish floating in this smaller tank. These were the fish that my father grew. He was waiting for them to reach sufficient weight so he could release them into the beautiful aquarium or *hòn non bộ* for Uncle's breakfast. Like a litter of pigs that were fattened to be sold in the market, the fish were grown for the day of their being eaten up by Uncle.

The fish swam in the small tank under the bed in the dark all day and every day. They were not cognizant of the passage of time as they imbibed the fish food that they were provided with regularly. They ate without even knowing what this meal actually was. Gradually, they forgot about vigilance and instinctual fear. There was no danger here in the dark tank. They probably learnt about boredom instead. They gradually grew to their full sizes without even realizing it. One day, though, suddenly, they were brought

out into the light and placed in a huge tank before the
statues of the folk gods, a portal to life. But ironically, at that
very moment they faced death at the hands of my Uncle!
They would soon receive the surprise . . . or rather the
shock of their lives. Uncle would be giving them a chance
to be liberated from the coils of this life. He would crush
them to extinction.

'Take it slowly', my father would caution him. Uncle
would swing his head wildly and his hair would appear long.
The balls of his eyes would turn white with excitement. He
would look at Dad and smile gently. He would then mutter
'Ok. Ok. I will eat slowly. No one eats in a hurry.' He would
dip his hand into the aquarium and stroke the gods.

'Their chess game is taking forever to end,' he
would remark.

My father would chuckle. 'How can anyone say that
your Uncle lacks humour,' he would challenge.

My father had a theory about why my Uncle was so
fond of eating raw fish. He insisted it was because my
grandmother was obsessed with the ocean when she was
pregnant with Uncle. These larger-than-life dreams got
transmitted to her belly and into the very lifeblood of the
baby. On occasion, when grandmother would relax over a
drink, she would recall her memories about the ocean—its
smell, its unceasing waves. Resting her head on the table,
tired and forlorn, she would find that her mouth was salty
and bitter, as though filled with astringent sea water. Even
when she was birthing my Uncle, the sound of the waves
echoed in her ears and she felt as though wet waves were
lashing against her dry face. Her soul burned with longing
for the sea. Even as the ball of fire with big spikes on its back

was ejected from her belly, it was as if a huge ocean wave had rolled out of her.

People are ruled by their obsessions. At first, I didn't take to this idea even though it held a strange fascination for me. But gradually, this idea grew on me. The proof to the claim of people being ruled by their obsessions is made evident by my grandmother's life. Till the day she died, her obsessions did not leave her. As she lay in bed wiping the sweat from her face with her hands, she would mumble, 'I am drenched in sea water. My body is filled with it.' She felt that the waves of pain that assailed her were like ocean tides that hit the shore, and as they did, they swept her along and her life ebbed gradually. Soon, she would melt away.

'It was your grandmother's obsession that injected this weird poison into your Uncle,' my father affirmed with certainty. 'This lethal dose did more harm to the baby than strangling it in the belly,' my father continued sadly. He was then jolted out of his reverie, 'Hey! That's an old story. There's no point talking about it anymore.' That was the first and last time my dad discussed this matter. His words were etched in my mind like a nail hammered to the wall, despite the fact that he had recounted this strange tale just once.

Father regularly caught fish. Every day, all his life he would leave a fish for my Uncle to eat. He was resigned to this, accepting it as the after-effect of the previous generation's eccentricity. Father bestowed on Uncle the great legacy of the sea by bestowing on him his daily fish. But my Uncle didn't understand the sacrifice. He just looked at the fish as he always did . . . as something to fill his stomach with. After his meal, he would get bored and would go to bed.

When he woke up, he went back to eating. It wasn't his lot to register the twists and turns of life.

One day, my father brought home a gargantuan fish. This was just after the drought. The rivers had returned to full spate and water rushed through them, bringing with them several large fish. The rivers were full of these huge fish that smelled like devils. That's correct . . . you heard me right, they did smell like devils. These fish looked and smelled like something being shadowed by demons. They jumped ashore and swam all over the waters in the flooded fields. This led to a surprising turn of events. The cracks in the parched lands disappeared as if they had never existed. The big swathes of yellowing, dried grass suddenly turned lush green.

For the first time, my Uncle had a huge mossy-green fish whose irises were clear. That's because it had had enough water and fresh air—nourished like a healthy young plant. As soon as it was placed in the aquarium, it thrashed around the two folk gods busy with their chess game, toppling them over. It jumped high and fell outside the huge fish tank. Uncle cheerfully picked it up to put it back in the fish tank, but it jumped out again. My Uncle was delighted by its size since it looked devilishly huge.

It also finally closed a painful chapter in our lives.

It was late afternoon. My father had gone to the field. Along with other children, I was playing 'chase' by the haystack. We were caught up in our game and I forgot to monitor Uncle as my father had instructed me to.

Meanwhile my Uncle was entangled in a deathly fight with the giant fish. He had no means of gauging its great strength. He misjudged its power. Instead of biting off its head, he sucked at it like a piece of candy. He slurped at it. The fish whacked him with its enormous tail and caught him unawares. With his throat bloodied, he lay dead when I came upon him. He had died while the fish was still alive as it slithered down his throat . . . all the way down. There, finally, death caught up with it as well.

When we children returned from our games, the sky above us had darkened ominously. Rimmed with black heavy, clouds, the firmament appeared to have prepared itself for an afternoon of mourning. It took many years for people to shut out memories of the way that dark, overcast sky had shrouded the garden on that awful day, or to cast out the image of the way poor Uncle had lain beside the aquarium. Such terrible memories take a long while to fade. Even now, when people sit under the haystack cheerfully singing a song or children play 'catch' chasing each other around it, it only takes a word or a phrase, uttered incautiously by someone to jerk the awful memory to the surface of the mind. Instantly, everyone feels a chill creep up their spine. They would then shiver and rush home. The tale affected everyone impartially, both children and adults.

People are haunted by dark memories. This tragic tale certainly haunted the community for over a decade . . . two decades even. Slowly, stories about the little fish tank under my father's bed also started emerging. There was much speculation about how my father had raised these fish, and how he had managed to discipline my Uncle into eating just one fish a day. But there was something about the little fish tank that no one knew, but us—my father and I. No one knew that after Uncle's death, my father completely forgot about the fish-tank under his bed. It was just there, totally unused and untended, with the multitude of fish swimming around in the same water, neither being fed nor cared for. Thus starved, they started eating each other in their desperation, each one eating its companion, gnawing it to the marrow.

They had turned cannibalistic, eating their own kind. Strangely, their facial structure changed, becoming thin and bony. Their teeth sharpened. As they swam around in the stinking tank with the residue of their companions' flesh, blood, and bones, they inhabited the harshest environment of their lives. Devoid of nourishment to sustain their lives, it became a game of the survival of the fittest. Finally, it was the most demonic, the slyest, most evil-looking fish that emerged the victor. It was the sole survivor, which meant that it had killed all its companions to survive . . . fifty in all, if we remembered correctly.

When the fish tank was finally found beneath the bed, we saw the face of this hideous fish. There was something extremely scary and spine-chilling about it. We had expected to see fifty dead fish floating in the tank or perhaps slightly less, assuming that the bigger ones had eaten the smaller ones. But to find just one fish swimming around in victorious solitude was a frightening sight. The fish, however did not seem to be in good condition. Its tail and fins were battered, perhaps in the battle for survival . . . or, had it tried to eat itself? There is no way of finding out.

We rushed to fling it into the river, pouring it out of the tank like humans drain out their fear—in a rush, not stopping to think. After returning home, the memory lingered, refusing to be banished from our minds. We thought of Uncle; recalled those mornings when with childlike eyes he would gaze at those fish. Father and I also drained the aquarium that had housed the gargantuan fish.

We no longer dare to dive, swim nor play in the river. It is so easy for us to imagine ourselves as sharing the same fate as the fish who were caught and trapped in the fish tank under our bed.

Translated from Nguyễn Ngọc Thuần.
Cha và con và . . . tàu bay.
NXB Hội nhà văn, 2005, pp. 149–157.

'My home' by Ha To Lam Anh

Ants Pursue Their Own Direction
(2009)

Đỗ Phấn (1956)

'*The butterfly and the dragonfly are the same as*
The fly, the ant, and the grasshopper.'
Bùi Giáng

She didn't understand why he had brought her to this
weird house. The smell of stale incense filled the air. The
ceiling looked as though it was going to cave in any minute.
Statues of Buddha, sitting and standing, filled the floor. The
statues, though plentiful, were all damaged. They exuded
the tragic horror of carnage. The gold flakes were off some
of them. The incense sticks that had been stuck randomly
in the crevices on the walls had burnt to the end, shedding
their ash to the ground. The empty sticks remained stuck
to the holes in the walls in an unseemly way. A swarm of
fire-ants leisurely made their way in and out of every little

crevice and fissure. As they moved around, they carried with them the soft, smooth glittering sand of their homes.

It's September . . . stormy season. Rain clouds had been gathering in the east all day long. The brackish yellow sun looked ripe and ready to flee. Intermittent flashes of light from the streetlamps lit up the street fleetingly. The sleepy, sultry street suddenly turned red, readying itself for the night.

At the intersection, a multitude of motorcycles jostled each other. There was no room to plant a foot on the road or even exchange a glance. In the midst of the exhaust fumes and the frantic din, her eyes were imprisoned behind the helmet's black visor. Frustrated by it all, she abruptly removed her visor as she sat behind the wheels. The sun had disappeared. The black visor attached to the helmet played its part in augmenting the darkness. All one could see in front was a sea of helmets. Like a bizarre collection of ant heads—smooth and round. These huge ants, however, were radiating exasperation and irritation.

The green traffic light came on. Sunglasses were pushed up noses again. Shiny, helmeted heads shook and wiggled. Engines roar. A group of motorcyclists follow each other in an unholy rush, looking a lot like fleeing ants. They spread out from the intersection. They had a minute . . . just one minute to flee the place. That was the sole aim of every motorcyclist there. She didn't make it, however. She didn't make it the next round either. It wasn't until the third time the green light came on that she was able to cross the intersection. How many intersections were left? Beneath the helmet, sweat trickled down her hair—salty.

She turned on the headlights. Ahead of her, she saw a wall of backs.

In a small apartment on the west side of the city, he sat waiting. He had been waiting since 4.00 p.m. He had been viewing and responding to text message on his cell phone. 'Please wait for me right there'; 'Don't give up on me yet, I'm on my way.' After having waited for yet another hour, he had texted back, 'Are you close to the house now?' But there was no reply. The message was probably lost in the maze of virtual networks. Perhaps the signal line was also heavily congested now. It was as annoying as the traffic congestion.

He gazed at the stack of old newspapers in front of him. News about cattle diseases and traffic accidents had occupied the front pages. He had been so bored reading about them. He shoved the stack deep under the chair. A swarm of flying ants that had nested there were dislodged as a result. The path of the ants, who had assiduously been moving something, was now blocked by the newspaper stack. The line of ants who had been moving in military regulation was now plunged in disarray. The ants who had been moving in a line on the door frame too were disturbed by a sudden lightning strike outside. They too broke formation and rushed down. A cold wind wafted by, moving the ants into greater chaos. In an instant, the whole floor was covered with ants. Some clung to small crevices on the door frames, often colliding with each other. White, speckled ant eggs fell over the corner of the door. They also fell inside the shoes that lay scattered near the door.

He was drawn to the hungry ants. He wasn't sure since when. Probably after reading an article that reported about how a mooncake factory hadn't realized that the cake was produced in Vietnam. The salesperson had insisted that the cake had been imported from Hong Kong, when, in fact, it had carried a minute stamp, as small as a fingernail, that had said that it was, in fact, produced in Vietnam. The information printed on it in minute letters—that needed a magnifying glass to decipher—carried all five ingredients as per the regulations of the food authority. Those letters had been tiny . . . smaller than wild ants.

The ants were in constant motion. They couldn't see each other but they somehow seemed to be effectively transmitting signals to each other to avoid obstacles along the way. He tried a little experiment. He applied a piece of transparent tape over one ant. Immediately, the ants behind split into two rows. They circumvented the tape and then merged into a single file again further on, even though you could clearly see the little fellow struggling under the clear tape.

On the wall next to the door, the ants were steadily making their way. They streamed along in two lines, one going forward and the other returning. But they didn't seem to be following the shortest path. Instead, their routes were rather convoluted. *Usually, the experiments undertaken in our country are about the same*, he thought to himself. *They record a phenomenon. Then wait until the next time the experiment is conducted, then record it again.*

Was the university where he had been teaching for the past twenty years been an experiment in progress? To assess students? Was it some kind of a test-device? Students sometimes believed that they were the successful by-products of experiments. But others were made to feel like they were failures. As for teachers . . . it could be worse.

They never really felt like they were achieving anything special. Yet, unfailingly, every year, they may have been voted as the best workers. Were they also just experiments... mere test specimens? Were they classified into serfs and lords? Into proletariat and bourgeoisie, into Sirs and Ladies, based on their status? Perhaps they were all specimens in the experimental laboratory of a more advanced life form? An extraterrestrial?

She rushed into the apartment with a bouquet of flowers and a lot of anger. They hardly had time for each other. She barely got to meet him once a week. They were getting on in life and were no longer in the first flush of youth. Surely, the 'old' can't afford to wait a week, each time! But there's not much point in getting angry with him. It's not his fault. Neither can she get mad at her fellow motorcyclists on the road—at the hundreds and thousands of bored faces beneath helmets that must all feel like her. Not much point in cursing them either.

He gazed up from his observation of the ants and looked rather bemusedly at the bouquet in her hand.

She looked down at him in equal bewilderment and asked, 'What are you doing sitting in a corner of the room by the door?'

'I'm starving ... starving,' he wailed.

She laughed. 'Just wait while I arrange the flowers,' she rejoined.

The rain followed only a few steps behind her entry. He closed the windows. The room became quiet suddenly, like a machine that had been shut down. He could hear the sound of running water in the bathroom and imagined the water gently caressing her silken skin. Peace . . . quietude!

She walked briskly out of the bathroom with her hair pinned up. In his hands, he held a vase filled with yellow roses, which he then handed to her. The vibrant colour of the flowers contrasted sharply with the dark fabric of the towel that she had wrapped carelessly around herself. The droplets of water making their way down her body shimmered like silver drops on dark petals. A buried memory of a woman like a faded flower invaded his mind that was tinged with fatigue, passion and regret.

He took the vase back from her hands and placed it with care on the transparent glass table. Tiny drops of water fell on the glass, glittering, and dancing like little imps.

She looked up into his smug face. It was dull, stupid. Deftly, he embraced her, his fingers touching the nape of her neck. He placed a slow kiss on her parted lips. She squeezed him . . . very tight . . . at the back. The dark towel that was wrapped around her, loosened. Her passionate lips roamed slowly over his. Slowly . . . seductively. He lifted her up. Placed her neatly between the cushions of the living-room chair. He knelt, pressing his ear to her heart. Rapid heartbeats. She pulled him on top of her. Passionate . . . sated . . .

The rain was persistently falling. The drumming of the raindrops against the glass door drowned out all other sounds, it drowned out the bustle of humanity from outside. There were no more human voices to be heard. No more sounds of cars. Everything had been shut out. She moaned softly—a sound of deep satisfaction. Not strident or bossy.

Who was he to have acquired a beauty and appropriated her in such a cavalier fashion? Was he a fiery hero? A yearning lover? Was he destined to endure anguish? Perennial delay? A passion greater than wished-for? Conflicting emotions clashed within him. Something broke. She squeezed her eyes shut. All her senses were calm. She was holding on to this precious moment.

Dinner was set for only two. One person plus another makes a love affair possible. But mathematics breaks down there. How can you add up a life plus another? What would that make? She narrated a conversation she heard from her roommate in her office this afternoon. It seems in Germany they were discussing the possibility of passing a seven-year marriage law. He raised his eyebrows in query. After seven years, it is proposed that the marriage automatically ends of its own accord so that, if you feel the need to continue with the marriage, you would have to get married all over again. Heavens! Another seven years of hope and despair!

Where is the question of success or failure in a marriage? When it ends, it ends with a loud bang. Look at him. Here he is. He's bought a small apartment in a long communal house. He had shamelessly carried around an unhappy face and parked it in the two tiny rooms, along with the ants. Tiny . . . yellow. The black ones are flustered. But all are defined by their silence.

She had mentioned some failed marriages. She never said more. They no longer matter. She said that she wanted to find sympathy and share in their relationship. Even empathy is possible given their circumstances. But sharing . . .? Well, he didn't think that was possible. He had nothing left to share.

She had bought takeout home to keep in the fridge. After a hasty shower, she arranged the flowers and completely forgot to put the food in the refrigerator. Then she remembered and walked in to lift the tray. She switched on the bright light outside the bedroom, only to discover long-legged black ants clinging to the paper wrapped around the food. Sensing the light and her presence, they ran frantically around at a speed that seemed to match her thoughts.

What would it feel like to have them crawl over her bare arms . . . over her sweaty breasts. . .over his chest . . . her neck . . . then up her face, those delicate legs dancing gracefully up the bridge of her nose. She screamed and quickly placed the tray of food on the glass table.

He laughed and calmed her down. He reassured her that he knew a way of solving the ant problem. He retrieved a gas lighter from his pocket and adjusted the flame to the maximum. The flame burned white. He pointed it near the food package. The ants rushed to the edge of the table and were crawling around it. Now he drew the flame near the edge and followed the ants all around the table with it. They began falling slowly to the floor. The flame crackled. There, it all ended.

She gazed at the angry ants crawling around on the floor. 'Why couldn't you just buy a bottle of ant-spray killer and finish them off?' 'You must be joking,' he said, 'people raise ants to relieve sadness, so how can I kill them?' 'You old man . . .' she remarked, laughing. 'Who, me? Old man?' he asked in a mock-angry tone. She laughed affectionately.

The morning rituals were always the same. She tiptoed out of the room to get dressed and opened the front door to go to the supermarket next door. She let him sleep deeply after the frantic sex of the night before that had more than made up for the long week of abstinence. She needed to buy some fast food and a few cans of beer for lunch at the lake since he had promised to take her a daytrip to the resort this morning. The lake district was only around a two-hour ride on the motorbike from home. She purchased the needful but decided to hide from him the can of ant-killer spray that she had also bought.

Last night, she had tried to close her eyes and wrestle with the feeling that she had swallowed an ant in the food and that it was lodged in her throat. She felt as though she could smell the stench of the ant on the tip of her nose. The salesperson had warned her to be careful with the spray. It had to be stored carefully away from children and she needed to ensure that they couldn't take it out and play with it since it was highly toxic. Well, there were no children to play with it, she thought comfortably. Suddenly, she remembered her son from her second marriage. He had been so naughty. Once, he had eaten an entire tube of toothpaste. Now, he was all grown up and stayed with her parents. He was now as gentle as a girl. She wondered if it was some delayed effect of the toothpaste. Well, what can one say? His father hadn't eaten any toothpaste. No wonder his personality hadn't softened! During their three-year marriage, his father had proven his worth as a man just once, when he had given her their son.

She returned home with her purchases. He had woken up and was taking a shower. He was singing in the shower again. The lyrics from a popular war-song assailed her ears:

'We crossed the high slopes of Truong Son mountain'. A heroic song. Everyone's favourite. She shouted over the sound of the shower, 'Let's leave early so that we can take advantage of the dry spell between the rains.' She heard him laugh in the midst of the shower. 'The more it rains the better it would be because then we can rent a cozy room in the motels along the way,' he replied.

'Utter nonsense,' she said laughingly. 'Remember there is one whole day to get through.'

Sporting a rather youthful-looking workout outfit, he left the house to get his motorbike from the parking lot. She deliberately lingered, waiting for him to disappear. Then, she hastily rummaged through his storeroom to look for the ant spray that she had hidden earlier and began spraying it . . . under the stove, near the door . . . everywhere. She covered her nose, closed her eyes, and sprayed. A pungent smell rose into the air. She dashed to the door and shut it deftly behind her. She turned the lock twice. Her face was pale like a thief caught in the act. She threw the spray in a public trash can and went in search of him.

They shoved the helmets down over their heads and blended in with the rest of the crowd on the streets, who were all wearing similar shiny, circular helmets as they swarmed the streets like bald ants. She yelled at the top of her voice; of course, only he could hear her.

'Slow down!'

'What for?'

'Coz I'm not sure if these new helmets are of good enough quality.'

'Maybe not but they have their uses. No one will recognize me and I won't recognize anyone either. We can all move about like ants in a swarm. This suits me. I'm really not into meeting anyone now. If I see an acquaintance and don't greet him, then they will remark that I've become very full of myself. So, I'd rather travel around like this . . . incognito.'

They got out of the crowded city through the bridge. The sun was high in the sky. By now the cars and motorbikes had reduced in number. She could smell the scent of the rice fields. She hugged him tight. The bike accelerated. The wind blew into her face even beneath the visor.

The lakeside resort was visible beside the lake in a small clearing. It looked lush and serene. The swallows had returned rather early in the season. As they sat quietly on the electric lines—that resembled subdued exclamation marks with their thin wings, lacking vitality. The several restaurants that skirted the lake resounded with the sound of brooms. The previous night's garbage was being pushed out into the street to form small mounds, waiting for the garbage van to clear them out.

He drove to the edge of the lake. She took out a plastic sheet and spread it on the grass. A few grasshoppers hopped onto the light-hued plastic sheet like brown rice husks. The season of lush green grass was over. It was now the locust season. These insects hide among the dead leaves and are not visible at first. One just hears the sound they make—'lok bok'— before they fall onto the sheet.

She doesn't like insects. They really freak her out and their scent really put her off.

'Don't you get the smell? For me, all the arthropods, like ants or bugs smell the same. The smell blocks my nose and makes it stuffy.'

In response, he shook out the plastic sheet and swatted all the locusts away. They flew around for a while and then settled. For a moment, the lawn appeared clean and there was no sound.

They both lay spread on the grass, gazing up at the sky. The dark, somber clouds gathering in the east signaled the long stormy season approaching in September. There was something unsettling about the quiet surface of the lake with its murky water. He stroked her hair and gently enquired:

'Besides ants and grasshoppers, what else are you afraid of?'

'Flies, especially in the vegetable gardens.'

'So, who breeds these flies?'

'Silly! Of course, it's the fly spawn!'

'Well, there was a scientist on TV the other day who claimed that it was people. He said, "Greed breeds flies".'

Surprised, she turned to look at him. 'Does everything come back to humans?'

'Pretty much. Overpopulation!' He paused a little and then continued, as though talking to himself. 'In "civilized" Japan, someone sprayed Sarin poison in the subways. Now, the smell of bugs and the smell of death pervades it. What about the human smell . . . your smell . . . my smell . . . and when we come together to make love . . . we emit another scent . . . the scent of reproduction.'

She wasn't mollified. She expressed her views harshly, saying that it was no surprise that he seemed so fond of that awful slum apartment in the city and stayed there alone, not progressing. He attempted to stem her words, 'Why is there this relentless need to constantly progress?' But where was the point? He knew it would never end well. It was the same story a few years ago but with another woman. So, he softened his voice, stroked her. They rented a room, stored their things there. He took her out to the street to enjoy and encountered some acquaintances there. Finally, she stood up rather sadly and reached for the two helmets. The locusts jumped out again and did a weird dance with their earthy, brown wings. She noticed their sick red bellies, which resembled sores on the flesh.

She doesn't understand why he has brought her to this strange place. The owner is the local antique dealer. An amateur. Absolutely! Dealing in antiques is a very strange profession. One might work in the business for generations but one was still only an amateur. Similarly, those dealing with heirlooms also never dared to call themselves 'professionals'. Their pride at never acknowledging their professional stakes came at a cost. Not at all like the fake painters who felt no reticence in talking about matters that they didn't understand.

Antique dealers dealt in secrets. So did the collectors. Neither dared to brag about their precious possessions. They would be questioned about their origins. In small towns, antique dealers sold items of obscure origins. The dealer was as quiet as the objects he sold. He carefully took out the rusty, ancient coins that had over time melded together. He also brought out a few shallow, ear-shaped, drinking cups (*nhĩ bôi*), some Chinese vases and a medley of old, bronze items.

He was looking at all the antique items closely and was trying to select one to buy. Just a small item. He always did this every time he passed by the antique shop, to commemorate the day.

She quietly asked him, 'Why are these statues of the Buddha strewn on the floor like this?' He laughed and replied tongue-in-cheek, 'They are bored to forever sit on the lotus in an exalted state. They want to integrate into the world to save all life forms.' She playfully kicked him on the back of his heel. He quickly warned her, 'Watch out, there are some fire ants.'

'What . . . ants again!' She was exasperated.

He looked downcast as he took her to the garden to see statues of dogs. The dealer didn't follow them out. The garden was full of various statues of dogs—some looking sad, some happy, some baring their teeth in anger. No two of them looked the same. They all had thoughtful, sometimes sad, expressions, which were carved into the stone. But it seemed to him that the sculptor's great talent, that was on display here, didn't really capture her attention. Or, was it just that she was too busy looking out for ant nests? She didn't comment either. When he persisted and said, 'Tell me, which one do you like?' She answered indifferently, 'When do you think this pile of rocks covered with mud and dirt will be properly cleaned?'

At noon, she refused to return to the lakeside picnic spot to have lunch as planned. 'Why should we go back to that place so full of flies and locusts?' He chuckled under his breath. In a way they were actually both rather similar. They couldn't be a couple. They were like two sandals meant for the same foot. She hated flies, ants and grasshoppers. He disliked crowded places . . . where flies and ants were usually found.

The restaurant was very crowded. On weekends the city dwellers would choose to sit under the pretty palm-leaf huts on the lawn outside. They both had to go inside into the air-conditioned dining hall. It was enclosed. The room was so noisy that they couldn't talk. He waved his hand and a waiter in a red vest, holding a menu card, walked over. They pointed their fingers at their favourite food items to order. She followed his movements like an automaton. There wasn't any choice.

Their food packs were still untouched. He rummaged through the bag to take out a can of beer to drink. They were still sitting in the air-conditioned room. It was like the beer shops in town. But he lost interest in drinking the beer. It was impossible to have a conversation in a place where there were already too many words being bandied around. Like a crowded beehive. Thousands of bees working together in the hive speak in one language . . . buzzing together . . . buzz . . . buzz.

After having eaten and drunk through the noise, he dragged her to the motel room. Their lovemaking in the afternoon wasn't particularly exhilarating. It was too regulated, each step followed through quickly as though completing a task. She wasn't as warmly responsive. She just lay there, open, receiving . . . but with a measure of uninvolvement.

They had reached home. It was dark. It started raining again. They still had time to park the motorcycle. But the rain started falling with greater ferocity as they jogged back to the apartment. Their clothes were damp by the time they made it inside. They unlocked the door. The toxic smell of the ant killer poured out of the door. She quickly turned on the light and opened all the windows and turned on the fan to full volume. Black and yellow ants lay everywhere on the floor, piled up against the walls. A few ants still lay squirming. She used a broom to sweep the dead ants out into the rain-soaked hallway. They stuck to the broom. She threw away the broom. He looked at her and saw her self-satisfied look. He felt so gutted. Where was the need to look so smug?

Ants didn't take up much space. They had been around for millions of years but unlike humans, they did not endlessly proliferate, annexing more and more of the planet's spaces, fighting with each other . . . trampling over others. He dreaded the thought of having a family with her . . .

The following afternoon, he sent her a text message. 'I'm going away. I'll not be there in my apartment. I've left the key next door.'

She texted back, 'Do you want me to kill the rest of the ants?'

He replied, 'No, all of them are already gone. Ants pursue their own direction.'

Translated from 'Kiến đi đằng kiến' in *Kiến đi đằng kiến và những truyện khác*. Hà Nội: NXB Phụ nữ, 2019, pp. 31–44.

'Butterfly' by Khương Hương

In the Editing Room (2005)

Nguyễn Bình Phương (1965)

The editor sat in front of his desk leaning back slightly. On the left was a disorderly pile of books donated by authors. A reading lamp painted in blue was lowered to shine on the reading materials. The editor's eyes were absorbed in the task of deciphering the handwritten manuscript as he diligently read, reaching the sentence 'the flames were rising proudly' when he was abruptly interrupted.

'May I have a minute of your time, please? I'm not sure what this word means.'

'Let me see,' said the editor.

'See this line here. I can't decipher this word. Can you help?'

'"A day bereft of sunshine with no shadows and with dragonflies hovering just above the ground that was lush with grass and full of flowers, as if they were ... something". Hmmm, not sure what precedes "something".'

'I'm not able to make out what the word is', the junior proofreader admitted.

'Can it be "as if they were looking for something"?'

'Looking?'

'Hang on, let me give this some thought. Perhaps it could be "dreaming". No, that won't fit. Moreover, it's too poetic for the context. But "looking for" is not very suitable either. It seems too facile.'

'What about the word, "thinking"'?'

'Thinking'? Well, erm . . . "dragonflies thinking" doesn't make much sense.'

'Well, who knows? Perhaps they can think?'

'Think? Dragonflies? Well, these days, it's rare to find even a human who can "think" let alone dragonflies. But it's rather strange that it is a dragonfly. Why not a cricket or a worm? Such a dearth of imagination. From the start to now, the author mentions the dragonfly dozens of times. Are we bold enough to edit out the insect and just retain the description of the grass and the flowers? That would make the passage much clearer and easier to read. That's worth keeping like love.'

'Dragonflies can't really be described as "flying", can they? Don't they, in fact, drift about? Surely, only birds 'fly' superseding all care . . . above fear. Of course, there must still be some fears that persist.'

'Well, what is your solution to this sentence?'

'Hmmm . . . wait a minute . . . it's like "they're getting angry". That might be it, dear girl. An angry dragonfly sounds most weird but it is in keeping with the writing style of the good old author. Okay. Let me read it over again . . . "dragonflies hovering just above the ground that was lush with grass and full of flowers, as if they were angry at something . . ." Does that sound okay?'

'Well, that's entirely up to you. You are the editor. I'm happy to insert whatever word you think is appropriate. As a proofreader, I just follow your instructions. Are you sure you want to choose that word?'

'Yes, yes, I agree. Let me ponder over this a little more. Anger is caused by a stimulation of the nervous system . . . it's a kind of shock. But what can dragonflies be angry about? No one bothers them. Why would they be angry? Why? Life is very complex and stressful that after I'm beset by worry, I daydream about my wife lying stretched out, passively, without expression, or I think about a huge meal. But anger is not an illusion. It's real. Illusions are like air bubbles that pop up and change positions in an impromptu manner. But coming back to dragonflies . . . we are not endlessly preoccupied by thoughts of them but when they are present, they do provoke some interesting speculations. "Looking…angry…dreaming…thinking… seeing…" Yes … it seems to me that perhaps "seeing" is the most appropriate word to use here. So, then it can signify a dragonfly hovering high and then low, wandering here and then over there . . . almost as if they were curious. As if there was something rather strange underground and they were auditing it . . . you know, like they were trying to probe it.'

'Well, you just have a fertile imagination! The ground is covered in "love grass", which is rough, bristly and very itchy. What fun can they derive from exploring it? You are assuming that they think like you.'

'Like me?'

'Well, who else has your curiosity, eh? Your hands are everywhere, grabbing, touching . . . '

'Come on! That happened just once but you go on about it forever.'

'Why shouldn't I? I will keep on saying it until you promise to not do it ever again.'

There was no one else in the room. The editor noticed her neckline was wide and low and her cleavage was just visible where there were two soft mounds. He felt hot and flushed and couldn't stand it any longer. He felt nervous as though his blood vessels would burst. Luckily, he didn't reveal his lust but held back, agonizing over this obsession he had with breasts.

'Well, I'm leaving now. So, it's agreed that I insert the word "explore" in the sentence?'

'Yes.'

'I think it is nonsensical but it's up to you.'

The door of the editor's office was never shut. It was always only half-closed.

If you peer from the office beyond the adjacent corridor, you'll see a series of brown shutters. There were no dragonflies there . . . simply because there was neither ground nor sky in that spot . . .

Translated from 'Trong phòng biên tập' in *Trí nhớ suy tàn và những trang viết khác* by Nguyễn Bình Phương. Hà Nội: NXB Văn học, 2005, pp. 144–148.

'*Hoa thuốc phiện* (Poppy flower)' by Khương Hương

Love Letter (2005)

Nguyễn Bình Phương (1965-)

Đoàn noticed that on the surface of the leather scroll-fragment that he had excavated a few months earlier, there now appeared to be some esoteric symbols. These were tiny, compact and strangely elusive—like light on water. Đoàn shut the door as he speculated about the analysis of this new finding.

Đoàn's wife, whose neck was as slender as her wrists, had just returned from the countryside. She took the opportunity afforded by his absence to brag to her neighbours. 'My husband is engaged in research. Most of you wouldn't have a clue. All I can say is that slander is easy but there are eyes above in the sky that watch everything.'

Đoàn strained to decipher the signs but wasn't successful. He decided to consult his friends. Dr Huyền was the first one to be called in. He took off his glasses and wiped them repeatedly on his trouser legs. Then, his eyes widening, he gasped.

'This scroll is most sacred. I don't think I'm learned enough to do justice to it.'

The linguist, Trịnh Tiến, who was trained in both classical Chinese and French, was more prosaic on being shown the scroll. He said that although he hadn't come across this type of writing before, in his opinion it was a letter. Glancing up at Đoàn and realizing that there was no objection forthcoming, Tien gained in confidence and slicing the air decisively with his hand, he asserted, 'This is a love letter.'

'Whose?' enquired Đoàn with narrowed eyes. Trịnh Tiến bit his lips, blinked and replied tentatively, 'Well, perhaps it was sent by a certain heroic general in Văn Lang's time to a celebrated beauty?'

'Hmmm . . . I wonder who that was.'

Đoàn's wife, who had been silently listening to this exchange, couldn't contain herself any longer.

'It looks a bit messy. I wonder if perhaps it's a map of some sort . . . .'

Đoàn looked up. He looked relieved and excited all at once. Slapping his thighs, he exclaimed, 'Of course! I'm such an idiot!'

Trinh departed rather shamefaced and Đoàn shut the door of his house decisively.

Late that night, when Đoàn lay sleeping, he dreamt that he was walking on all fours, his tongue was hanging out and he was panting like a dog. Sleeping beside him, Đoàn's wife heard her husband periodically make rhythmic whistling sounds as he dreamt.

The next unlikely man to swarm into Đoàn's house to attempt to decipher the specimen was Khang, who was commonly held to be crazy. Khang often stood in the middle of the street and sang out loud. Đoàn's dog looked at him with eyes that held panic. Khang smiled blandly, took the specimen, and quickly said, 'Allow me to see this.'

Đoàn jumped up in annoyance. 'Fuck off', he said vituperatively.

'Well, I'm not leaving. What are you going to do?'

Khang stood there unmoving asserting his stand with confidence. He then pulled out a chair and glancing briefly at his host, he turned to examine the scroll.

'I can comprehend it.' He remarked.

Đoàn looked bewildered. Although Khang was widely considered crazy with a face that looked haggard, his eyes were bright and alert and his voice strangely confident. Khang took up a pen and began translating, 'Dear beloved, I write these lines conscious of my helplessness. I have fallen in love. Yes. I'm deeply in love like a . . .'

Holding aloft Khang's translation, Đoàn read through it silently.

It took a long time for Đoàn to ask a question and his limbs were trembling.

'Where did you learn to read this script?' He asked.

'There is no need for me to learn,' Khang mumbled, took off his shirt, and left the house abruptly. The dog barked in a persistent, angry, frenzied, and resentful bout of vocalizing.

Đoàn's wife seemed to be greatly affected. She fell to the ground in a faint.

A fortnight hence, people saw Đoàn wandering around in the streets, his beard and hair growing unchecked, his mouth crooked.

'Dear beloved, dear love, I'm writing these lines . . .
I have written them bow wow. . .after realizing . . . yes, love,
like a . . . bow wow . . . Dear beloved, dear love . . . I'm
writing these lines . . .'

Đoàn sounded like a record stuck in a groove. Children
who saw Đoàn shouted, 'Let's run away, this guy is crazy.'

This could surely be one version of the truth.

But I, the author who penned this story, know another
truth. I cannot help wondering why that day, Đoàn's family
dog approached his master's table, looked around, and then
leaning forward, he moved his front paw and took hold of
a pen to write on the leather. It wrote most vigorously and
energetically letting out an occasional frenetic howl. After
a brief stint of writing, the dog appeared to lose steam. It
appeared bitter. Pulling its tail tight, it laid its muzzle on the
broom handle. Closing its eyes, it lay in contemplation all
afternoon.

The dog has a rough, gray coat and sullen, desolate eyes.

Translated from 'Trong phòng biên tập' in *Trí nhớ suy*
tàn và những trang viết khác by Nguyễn Bình Phương. Hà
Nội: NXB Văn học, 2005, pp. 99–203.

'*Con trâu*' by Khương Hương

Market Day in Giát District (1988)

Nguyễn Minh Châu (1930–1989)

1

The old man, Khúng, woke up with a start for he had had a nightmare. In his dream, he had a vision of an old man who was tall, with a bony structure, and part of his salt-and-pepper hair was short and spiky, which stuck out of his scalp as stiff as bamboo roots. But another part of it was a tangled mess, falling to the right and centre of his forehead. He had a pitted, rough face with angry eyes. Patches of an ox's blood, both damp and dry, stuck to the bulging muscles of his biceps and his shoulder blades. This frightful old man stretched out both his hands and lifted a large hammer that belonged to the head-smith of the Khơi village. He brought it down hard on the head of the ox. The terrible blow of the sledgehammer hit the ox on its forehead close to its eye and made the bloody eye pop out. He suddenly realized to his horror that this was the ox that belonged to Old Khúng (himself)—the 'black one' in his household, whom he had fondly dubbed 'the old woman who snorts', 'the sickly ox', the 'captain lady' of old Khúng's household. When she was hit, she bellowed with pain. The sound was horrific and appeared to emanate at dawn from a house in Cầu Giát Street.

From when he was young, Lão Khúng had to fetch firewood and for this he needed to walk through the abattoir, and he could not abide the sight of the killing of animals. So, he would cover both his ears and, with his feet, would take flight. He was generally not a squeamish kid. In fact, he was quite a sturdy, even fierce kid. But one thing he could not stand since childhood was the sound an animal made when it was in its death throes.

The question arose in his dream, 'Who killed the old man's black ox? His mate, his friend? Which accursed old man, which ungrateful son-of-a-bitch, which thief? Was he from the village or the mountains?'

Well, he got his answer. 'It was you, old man!' The perpetrator of the evil act was none other than old Khúng himself. It was with his own hands that he had raised the hammer to administer the death blow. When the realization hit him, his hands and feet began trembling. Sweat poured down his shirt and the old man became frightened. He had become so cruel. Since when had he become so imbued with evil . . . beyond human imagination? If he had been like many others who obey religious edicts, surely by now, at midnight, he would have promptly fallen on his knees, hastily recited the sacred verses and banged his head on the ground, pleading with the god he worshipped to forgive him, all the while pouring out his heartfelt remorse.

Being an atheist, however, old Khúng could only turn over and sit up on a wooden plank—trembling, lonely, penitent and alone in his suffering—in fear of his own self. He opened his eyes wide and encountered the ferocious 'butcher-god' who had just entered his body while he was sound asleep, lying peacefully on the familiar floorboard in the middle of his house.

It was then that he realized, like one who had narrowly escaped a great calamity, that this was just a nightmare. Old Khúng breathed a huge sigh of relief. *What luck! It was only a dream.* None of it was real. He could hear his old black ox snorting outside in the barn behind the kitchen.

Once again the old man settled down to sleep peacefully. He was already looking forward to his next dream. 'Honk! Honk!' That was strange! Why was his cow honking like a car horn? But it turned out that it was, indeed, a car. His ox had disappeared from his dream to be replaced by a majestic limousine that appeared from behind him. The rounded back of the car, however, didn't glide smoothly over the road but instead flew over the fields of sweet potato and bumped over the irrigation canal in front of his house. It then flitted over the lime yard, its four wheels not touching the ground. Eyes wide, behind the steering wheel, he saw a large man with a face as red and round as the rising sun. He was wearing a half-sleeved shirt, the colour of scrambled eggs. He was sporting a gray hat. This man smiled cheerfully at Khúng gesticulating in the air, emulating the gesture of leaders on stage that Mr Khúng had noticed several times in a movie. He recognized the man behind the wheel to be Mr Bời, the secretary of the Party District Committee, who was famous since he constantly appeared on radio and was quoted regularly in the papers. He was a close friend of Mr Khúng.

Though preoccupied with the dream until then, Khúng abruptly dismissed it from his mind. He remained in the same prone position, straightening his legs, his whole body softening slightly. For a long time now, he had had fleeting thoughts about death. Caught in the coils of his nightmares, he felt that there were few things to be happy about while there were risks and disasters everywhere. So, everytime he woke up from a dream, he always felt relieved, even happy. The real world, full of hardships and intimacies, first returned to him through his keen hearing. At the moment of awakening, he heard the sound of two dew drops that fell on the banana leaf boat next to his house and on the papaya tree behind the house. Old Khúng's two wise dogs remained silent.

Lying in bed, he could still hear their footsteps as they patrolled the yard, while the rest of the dogs in the neighbourhood were barking. As he lay listening to their distant barking—as though they were chasing a soul that was on its way to the graveyard, a soul that was changing from an embodied human into a ghost—he calculated that it was probably pre-dawn, around two or three in the morning. The numerous lights and machines at the large construction site in Đá Dầu valley had all been turned off. The night was dark and silent. It had been a long while since old man Khúng had been shrouded in such stillness at night. It brought on an atavistic fear in him as though he had been thrown back to his dirty little village, where he was born. Knowing that he would never be able to go back to sleep, old man Khúng attempted to sit up. However, a melancholic, heavy feeling pulled him down as though his body had been tied by a long, invisible rope to the very entrails of the earth. But as one who was a hunter and thus used to challenges, he determinedly sat up. Today, he had to go to the Giát Market to sell his ox. He was determined to lead the ox to the market as soon as he could.

All his life, among the many things that had plagued him with a sense of inadequacy was his inability to order the thoughts in his head and express them in words, even if it was only to himself. This assemblage of confused, sad, contradictory ideas that were so prickly and difficult to articulate, were like an ill-assorted herd of cows that had come together from many households and had been crowded into a cage all night, where they rammed and wrestled each other through the night. He felt that his head was right at the center of this narrow, confined cage. He sat up on the tarpaulin and immediately dropped his bare feet on the freezing floor. He did this with great resolution and decisiveness as if to signal that he was determined to overcome any lingering reluctance that he might have in carrying out this important task, which was indeed a duty that he had to perform this morning.

Resting a hand on the edge of his bed, he peered into the darkness. He noticed a child lying near the mouth of the rice mill, near the door that connects the outer and inner portions of the house. The old man realized that the child was Bút, his youngest son, only six. The crazy lad slept near his father's bed, on the floor outside, every night. But in the middle of the night, he had a habit of wandering off to snuggle into bed with his mother. At least that was his intention. But the lad often walked in his sleep and midway tripped over a sleeping dog, fell down and slept hugging the dog until morning. In fact, there was rarely an occasion when he had actually reached his mother's bed. In the morning, he was not to be found sleeping either on the bed or on the floorboard. One day, he would be found hugging the hand rice-grinder and the next, a broom. Like two diligent patrolmen of the yard, the two dogs remained silent, kept watch and paced the floor. The star-filled sky was heavy with clouds, shining and wet. Late at night, dew had fallen heavily from the leaves to the ground, that was now wet.

Old Khúng resembled an ancient, dried-up tree trunk, full of knots and twists. He stood silent and unmoving in the middle of the white-lime courtyard that faced the sea. He, too, was facing the sea. This was in the direction of the Khơi village, where his placenta and umbilical cord still lay buried along with the graves, where his forefathers were laid to rest. As he faced the direction of his ancestral village, the horizon appeared misty and blurred, and to his keen, listening ears, as sensitive as an animal's, came the murmurs and whispers of the waves of his homeland and his ancestors' graves. He had no means of knowing whether these were actual sounds or whether they were inner echoes that came back to him since he had first heard them in his mother's womb.

The old man stooped and walked briskly to the kitchen. His hands groped around in the dark recesses of the kitchen, where the strong, sour smell of pig bran mingled with the smell of goat dung and permeated the air. But these were familiar smells and so he did not even notice them. He pulled down two coils of rope, one new and the other old from the bamboo shelf high up in the kitchen. The kitchen was as dark as an underground cave. So, it was only through the feel of his hands that he could make out the coiled ropes. He had no intention of decorating the ox that he was about to offer for sale at the market the following day. Just by feeling with his hands, the old rope felt stringy and tattered. Also, even to his accustomed nose, the smell of animal sweat that had oozed out from it while plowing seemed to have seeped into the old rope.

Old Khúng had known for a long time now, indeed from the beginning of last year, that the black ox was getting far too old and weak. Even his neighbours, he was certain, had noticed it since last year and had remarked on it among themselves though none of them had said anything to him or his wife.

The ox had shriveled up like an old woman. But perhaps that was because the rope was old? It could be that because of this the cow looked even older and more decrepit? As old Khúng stood in the dark, he was busy debating the assets and liabilities of his ox when he presented her for sale in the midst of the busy market the following day.

As he stood in the dark, Old Khúng looked at the rope that had tethered so many oxen in his lifetime. It had been connected to the soil and sand of his house and had been a part of his life. Once, a long time ago, it had been a brand new rope with fresh bamboo fibers that were as glossy as silk that he had brought back home from Cày market along with his new black ox. He had used this very rope to tether his ox to bring it home from that very busy cattle-market. He had taught that stingy cattle trader a sharp lesson; and had indeed made no bones about embarrassing him in front of an audience when the trader had tried to remove the rope to only sell him the ox. He still remembered the man vividly—holding a large stack of rolled-up currency notes in his hand that looked like a *khăn xếp* (traditional Vietnamese head gear). What was he thinking! Did he expect the buyer to tie the ox to the drawstring of his trousers and lead it home? The rope had definitely looked very new, much newer than the new rope that Mr Khúng was holding in his hand right now.

As he thought about the bargain of the new rope, old Khúng went back to replace the new rope in the kitchen shelf and take out the old rope instead. Well, even if it was only a trifle, you had to pay for it out of your own pocket. No one gave you anything free of cost, he thought, as he walked across the paved pathway that led from the kitchen to the barn. As he passed the broken water-jug, which had been filled from the well, he took a coconut shell and scooped out some water to gargle. The black ox had seen him from the moment he had woken up, walked across the yard to the kitchen and had stood urinating for a while into the mound of ash behind the pigsty. Even on a dark night, the ox had no problem recognizing the old man even from afar. For over a decade now, the animal had become accustomed to the man standing on two legs like a wild plant that springs up from the ground.

Just taking a few short sniffs of the air, the ox could detect the familiar smell of old Khúng—his salty sweat— even from a distance. It awakened in the animal's mind a desire for obedience as if in tune with some inner prompting. Even as it saw the old man wiping the water with his sleeve and walking towards the barn door, the ox began pressing its hooves to the ground to stand up. But it was also like a child, much loved and pampered, knowing that he could take the liberty of being a little laid-back and lazy. Old man Khúng appeared to acknowledge that too. He placed his hand gently on its neck and obeying that command, when the oxen obediently rose to its feet, old Khung's hands trembled as he looped the noose around the animal's neck.

Old Khúng knew that this was the final knot. This time it would never be untied. He was tethering the ox to death. The withered, ancient ox didn't see the single tear that rolled down the old man's cheek to fall on the dry grass beneath his feet. The old man leaned over, stretching his arms out to nudge the bolt to its side to open the barn door for the ox to exit. With the old rope looped twice around the horn and hanging down one shoulder, which was as tough as a toad's skin because it had carried the yoke of the plow all its working life, the old black ox walked out of the barn, its four hoofs stamping hard on the powdery sand dried up during the hot summer months, covered with straw and with a scattering of fresh grass. A few steps out of the barn, the animal stopped and snorted, taking in the scent of damp earth and the night dew including the pungent smell that arose from the freshly-cut grass that had been tightly packed and tied up with a metal wire by Nghiên, Khúng's youngest daughter, who had cut it from the foot of the mountain at dusk the previous day. The ox stretched out and curled its leathery tongue around a sheaf of grass to rip at it and store it in its mouth to munch lazily with its white teeth as it repeatedly stamped its four hooves on the ground, as though to convey its displeasure and shock at being disturbed so early by the old man, for it was clear that it was still pre-dawn. Why was old Khúng pulling out the plow so early? As was its habit each morning before embarking on its daily duties in the field, the old black ox raised its snout to the sky and bellowed aloud its frustration at full volume, a sound that carried through the night.

As was his custom every day before the ox went to the field, old Khúng ran to pick up a large bamboo basket covered with ash and dried cattle dung and placed it between the hind legs of the ox. Ever since it had been just a calf, nearly fourteen years ago, the old man, looking at the butt of this old sucker could tell that he would excrete dung all the way to the field. The old man always ensured that he never wasted the dung. Since the base of the tail is not round but flat like the head of a bottlefish, the ox would reward him for his labour. The droppings were always firm with the right consistency. Never loose or semi-solid. The old man stood in front of the barn absently gazing at the stars in the night sky waiting for the dung to emerge, regretting that this would be the last day his family would avail this rich source of manure to pour into the compost pit. When he smelt the dung just falling out of the ox still warm and soft to the touch, the smell wafting in the air at this slightly chilly hour, the old man led the ox loosely by the end of the rope to the tree stump outside the narrow alley, when an ox cart rigged up with car tyres was stationed near the kitchen entrance with its slightly protruding beam. Here a foot-operated rice grinder was to be found and the two wheels of the cart were tied with a wire to its base.

Old Khúng observed that a pile of firewood and a bundle of green tea leaves had been loaded onto the cart.

He spied a head covered with a black scarf huddled on the other side of it. He was taken aback to see that his old wife Huệ had probably woken up around the same time as he had with the intention of bidding a final farewell to the ox. Mrs Huệ kept her counsel. So did he. He stood aside a little as she approached and took one of the ox's smooth horns in her hand and led the animal to the other side to drink from a vessel in which she had poured sticky rice porridge.

The old man went round the cart securing the rattan ropes that were tied to the bundles of firewood. He then went to the tree stump of the satin-ash tree and squatted down, holding the long fluted bong between his knees. His fingers appeared to be numb and they were trembling long before he could light the cheroot and plug it into the fluted bong—that was made of bamboo. He gazed around for a while before turning on the lighter. He tried to cover the flame with a bit of his shirt so that the light wouldn't shine inside the house and wake the children up at this early hour. However, the light was reflected in the rich brown earthenware water-container like a white moon. Mrs Huệ sat quietly while the ox happily slurped on the delicious sticky rice porridge that she had painstakingly prepared over long hours. It stuck its long tongue out periodically to savour it. This whole ritual had the makings of a party before the gallows. The old ox ate slowly, its neck bent down, almost motionless. Only its lower jaw was moving ever so slightly as from time to time the animal would bring its rough tongue to lick the sides of the vessel and then would lovingly lick Mrs Huệ's hands, reddened and rough due to a lifetime of hardship, straining to hold the earthenware jar with the porridge.

As she waited for the ox to finish eating, Mrs Huệ put out her hand still sticky with the rice porridge and stroked the ox several times. Old Khúng went over, threw his bong on the pile of green tea leaves, then bent down to lift both thills off the ground and attached the worn wooden yoke to the ox's neck. The old couple stood to one side gazing at the ox then at each other for a while in the sparse light of the deserted night. Neither spoke. Old Khúng knew that he had no more use for the ox. He also knew that he didn't need to persuade his wife about the need to sell the ox. But he didn't want to confront his son, Bút, nor his daughter, Nghiên. If these two saw them, they would jump out of bed straight away. He didn't put it past Bút—the stubborn chap—to stretch himself out full length in front of the cart, even clutching the front legs of the ox refusing to let go, preventing his father from taking it anywhere. Nghiên, his daughter, though only nine years old, knew how to wield a sickle for she worked hard every day, cutting grass, and bundling it up, carrying a full roll of turf. So, she ate well and was strong. One day, she went to cut grass in the ravine bordering Diễn Châu district. However, carrying the heavy roll of cut turf, she couldn't find her way back. She wandered around the mountains, both tired and hungry until nine at night, when she finally found her way back to the villa.

Keeping such thoughts at bay, the old man climbed hastily into the cart and sat precariously on its side calling out firmly, 'Hey, hey'. The ox didn't even wait for the old man to call out. It stretched out its neck as it pulled the worn-out tires and rolled over in front of Huệ, who was standing silently at the foot of the tree. After leaving the house and riding along for a while, he nimbly jumped out because the deep slope that came up made the cart roll by itself.

Old Khúng stumbled along, his hands holding on to the cart to slow its progress. He turned his head to look at the house as though it was the ox looking back for the last time at the house with its white triangular sloping wall, stamping its distinctive presence with confidence. The stars were beaming their lights down from a starry sky. He was stunned to see that it was not just his wife standing by the side of the house but a smaller shadow, his daughter, Nghiên. *When had she woken up? How had she known?* Old Khúng felt his heart hammering with anxiety.

From the afternoon of the day before yesterday, through all of yesterday and last night, old Khúng and his wife had agreed to keep from the children their decision to finally sell their ox. However, it was evident that their daughter had somehow sensed this decision and had woken up in time to bid farewell to the ox. Her palms were scratched and often bleeding because of the hard task of having to cut grass every day to feed the ox before putting it to the plow. In fact, most days, she woke up very early, even before her father, and it appeared that last night she had not slept at all. Her puny, undernourished body had only begun shedding her milk teeth at nine years instead of at seven. With the precocious maturity and wisdom that comes with great poverty, she realized that her family had no choice but to sell their beloved ox to get sufficient money for her father to build a house for her older brother, Lạc and his wife in Dak Lak. They were residing in the 'new economy zone', and were having difficulty meeting the terms. Dak Lak . . . Dak Lak . . . the name sounded foreign to the girl. It was beyond her ken, alien to her peaceful, humdrum existence. She had developed a quiet affection for her brother and his caring wife, as gentle as the earth, who was more a daughter of the family than a daughter-in-law. She had grown to love her and was the closest to her in the family.

In January last year, old Khúng had gone to visit his son in Dak Lak. He thought about his life and his son's, now and again, and felt sad. In his own lifetime, he had had no choice but to relocate, to leave his village and the graves of his ancestors near the coast to make his life here in this strange land of toxic water and dense forest. The soil was sandy for the most part. His life had been one long struggle with this barren land. But he had finally managed to find some temporary reprieve through taming the wild weeds. This strange, barren land had now been converted to somewhat familiar terrain. His toil had injected some fecundity to the parched land and his toil and sweat had watered the barren ground making it gradually more fertile. But now, after all this effort, his son had had no choice but to abandon this region to relocate to another, even more remote, more obscure, forested terrain.

Was this to be his life? Was this his destiny and his children's fate too? Was their fate to be no different to his? Old Khúng reflected sadly that if it hadn't been for the fact that he had to help out his son to begin his hard life in a foreign land, he wouldn't have had to make this trip to Giát market in the dead of night. The black ox was old. He had no clear idea how old, only that it still had eight teeth left. But it had been old for a long time. It was his unflagging care that had kept the ox in good health. It all depended on one's use of the animal. Mr Bởi, the Party District Secretary, was right in saying that in the communes, if there was an ox that was fat or thin, you just sent it to Mr Khúng in the highlands to care for it, and lo and behold, in just half a year, the ox would look youthful again and would be strong enough to wield the plow.

Suddenly, old Khúng saw a small shadow as slight as a blade of grass flit across the night, spurting out from below the huge tree that stood like a sentinel before old Khung's house. 'Stop! Stop!' He gently exhorted the ox in a quiet voice like he would to an old friend of many years as he held the cart wheels tightly reined in with his hands holding the ropes taut. Old Khúng stood waiting rather nervously for his daughter to catch up, and in the dark, he also made out their two family dogs, Dark Ink and Yellow, running ahead of her. Strangely, the two dogs had also become so attached to the ox through the years. They ran around its legs. These two watch dogs sniffed at the animal affectionately as though bidding farewell. But Nghiên just stood still, weeping. Her eyes were heavy with tears and they fluttered shut. She sat down on the ground in her rumpled *váy yếm* (tunic). Her short hair, bleached red by the sun that she hadn't yet tied up since getting out of bed with the *cặp ba lá* (three-leaf clover) hung all around her face and around the neck of the ox in a dishevelled manner as she hugged it. Her two small hands unceasingly stroked the head, nose and snout of the ox. Had the ox by now sensed through its sound animal instinct that this trip, undertaken in the dead of night, would be the last one of its life? Was it sad too? Unable to bear her sorrow heightened by her proximity to the animal that she had tenderly cared for all her young life, she ran over to her father and buried her face in his chest because she knew that he shared her suffering about having to sell the ox which their circumstance was forcing them to.

Old Khúng stroked the slender neck of the precious daughter of the family, who was so hard working. Soon, she ran from him, still crying, back to her mother standing silently by the tree. His daughter's hair and breath had smelt of the fresh grass of the fields. This smell to him was both bitter and sweet. The smell of crisp, dewy grass and the scent of the wild forest that rose from her young body aroused long-ago memories that had been dormant within him for many years. It took him back to the time when as a young man Huệ and he had just come to the highlands from Khoi village, struggling to make a life for themselves in this wild country. At that time, Nghiên had not yet been born. Indeed, more than half of his children had still been unborn and the black ox, which he had procured from Cáy market had no doubt still not even been conceived. It seemed to him that those long-ago days belonged to another age, as though, then, human beings had just been newly hatched. In those days, embedded in the heart of this wild country, his wife and he had only had their three older sons, Hùng, Dũng and Lạc. Indeed, Lạc had just been two months old. He had been a small, flushed bundle lying on his mother's lap.

Back then, there was dense forest in this region. There were only a few scattered settlements of humans. Some would say, far too few. Old Khúng's family was one of the very few who had dared to volunteer to settle here. However, ironically, there was more fear now than there had been at that time and it was not fear of animals—not of leopards, pythons, or tigers, especially since the days when a government construction site had been erected in these parts. The real fear these days was of other people. In those days, what was forgotten remained so with no repercussions. Even a new cotton shirt bought to wear in the summer would be carelessly stowed away in rock crevices in the cold season and would remain there all winter. No one would take it. Who was there to take it?

He had lived like a wild man, losing all facets of his personality that had defined him in the plains, as a farmer in the village. His wife who was city-bred had changed even more radically. Both had become very taciturn. Their personalities had blended with the forest. They had become one with the wild, almost. One day, when old Khúng saw his children playing together in a rock cave at the mouth of a stream, something in him had been scared and he had burst into tears and blurted out, perhaps in folly, that he wondered if his children were human or offspring of wild beasts . . . of civets, foxes and pythons.

Every time such thoughts troubled his mind, he would dismiss them as foolish and laugh aloud, alone, like a madman sitting in the midst of a wilderness so profound that he thought he could never escape it . . . that it had penetrated him completely. Gradually, the humans had outnumbered the animals. Iron had come to outnumber trees. Yet his anxieties had not lessened. Last winter, some labourers who were mechanics had stolen the yield from a whole field of newly ripened tomatoes, that he had painfully cultivated. More drastically, just last month, Hương, his daughter who attended the district high school and who was famed for her beauty, was to return home on Saturday for the weekend. It was barely dawn and he had been squatting on the front porch half-intent on baking a pot of sweet potatoes, when, looking up through the smoke that was diffused around the surrounding space, he was suddenly shocked to see his daughter running for her life as though chased by a wild animal. She was running barefoot as if her sandals had been flung off in her rush to escape, and her face looked pale and bloodless. He had been furious and had trembled with rage . . .

2.

Old Khúng now attempted to lead the ox that was yoked to the cart away to the market. But he hadn't made much headway because the cart was still at the bottom of the mound in front of his house. The powdery, sandy earth came almost to the calf of the ox and as the fine grains flew up, they cast a white haze ahead of him. All around him the ground was littered with piles of iron rods or coils of steel. These were interspersed with tall wooden containers the size of houses. Old Khúng was forced to jump down from the cart to safely navigate the ox and the cart through this forest of industrial waste that covered his path. Black Ink, his eccentric dog was still jogging alongside the cart. The old farmer stopped, jerked his whip in the direction of his house and made a hawking sound. The dog immediately picked up his cue and ran back to guard his house.

As dawn stretched, the sky and earth took on a strange glow. The rough trail of smooth soil with undulating slopes on both sides was buried under the growth of grass and myrtle. At this time of night, there was a slight chill in the air. The cold air appeared to have been shot down straight from the bright silvery stars scattered across the black sky.

He stretched his hand behind his back and grabbed the dull-gray coat that Huệ had thoughtfully stuffed among the bundles of firewood right behind where he was seated. 'Oh well! For Heaven's sake . . .!' He stopped his sentence halfway and remained silent, not willing to admit even to himself that he had foolishly made the ox leave the house far too early. He could have easily allowed both the animal and himself to sleep in a little more and left later. All of a sudden, old Khúng felt like a sneaky thief at night, stealing someone else's ox and he was annoyed with himself. It was also because of this ox that he hadn't managed to get any peaceful sleep at night . . . staying up late, falling asleep at midnight only to wake up with a start dreaming of it.

Slipping on the coat over one shoulder and sitting slouched against the wall of the cart, he gazed blindly at the rough, hairless neck of the ox over which the yoke had been placed and fastened. The cart tumbled along making rattling sounds in the pitch-black darkness of the night. It was a dark so intense that it felt as though it had been nailed to the front of the cart, too deep, too dense to penetrate. Beneath the plodding ox, Khúng felt that even the worms slumbering under the grass did not murmur. All the earth and the trees were silent at this hour as though gripped by a death-like sleep. Only the insects were chirping far away. The four sides of heaven and earth seemed to be enveloped in a darkness akin to that of the underworld.

Seated alone in the cart, old man Khúng was thinking ahead to the time when he would have to confess the sale of the black ox to his nine children from Bút, his simple youngest son to young Huong, studying in Grade twelve down in Cầu Giát Street, to Đoan, his son and Lê, his daughter, both of whom attended school for half-a-day and spent the rest of the day working with their old parents at home. He would also have to inform Dxng and his wife who were in the province and Lạc and his wife living in Dak Lak.

He felt desolate since the entire childhood of all his children and the attendant hard labour of the family were linked to the ox. They used to herd it and play with it. Working hard, plowing, harrowing the field, working late, waking early, this ox had become part of their family over the past eighteen years. It had taken him all this time to understand this obvious fact. 'Hurry up!' Old Khúng shouted suddenly in an angry voice. 'Hurry Up! Step it up quickly so that you can die as soon as possible. Let the hammer strike you down soon, you fiend!' After that, he would have to find a way to break the news to his sons and daughters . . . that from now on, the ox was no longer a member of the family, that he, Khúng, had killed it. he would have to convince his family that the animal was already old and decrepit, not young or a calf any longer.

Looking sadly at the ox, he thought, *this is your fate! For a lifetime of hard labour, you are rewarded by being killed for meat when you get old.* Had anyone let an ox die of old age to be sent off with a big funeral?

In the midst of that dark, silent night, only the silvery stars flickering in the sky stretched across the firmament of this vast world would have had an opportunity to see two fat teardrops sliding down the corner of Khúng's eyes. At that time, Old Khúng was silently communing with his second son who had been killed in the war with Cambodia two years ago, conveying to him wordlessly about his intention to sell the ox to Dũng. After the deep sorrow that he suffered at his son's death, which had enveloped him like an ocean that swoops in to cover the land that even after receding, leaves behind a salty debris that destroys the potatoes and rice plants, his suffering too had left him enervated, apathetic, not interested in working as he had been earlier. He realized then that he would have to live with this grief caused by his brave son's demise for the rest of his life.

Only his wife, Mrs Huệ, fully understood his feelings. He thought back to that afternoon two years back, when it had already begun to get dark. Only old Khúng and the black ox remained working beside a square mound of stones that was close to a newly discovered quarry in the Đá Dầu valley. The old man had scolded the animal at that time since it appeared unwilling to drag home the cart piled with stones.

'Why are you so lazy today? Do you think I'm not hungry? Pull the cart and let's go home,' he had said.

But he had uttered these words without rancour, lightheartedly. Old Khúng only teased the industrious, hard-working ox. It immediately and obligingly stretched out its neck, pressed down all its feet and determinedly pulled the cart away even as old Khúng hurriedly threw in a few more large stones as big as rocks into the cart already piled high with stones. He hoped to carry as many stones as possible in a few afternoons to mend the wall behind the kitchen that was broken. But strangely, the ox was acting up on this particular day. This was rather unusual. Old Khúng kept walking directly behind the cart, troubled all the while, sometimes with his hand automatically reaching out to support the ox when the heavy cart swayed from side to side or buckled a little when it passed the place where there was ankle-deep water. The thick bushes on either side had already begun to be shrouded by the gathering darkness.

The old man and the animal had barely reached the end of the road when they heard the loud crying and the lamenting that rose from the house. The cries were full of deep and terrible pain. There was no light anywhere in the house, neither in the kitchen nor upstairs. That minute, something crashed and died within the old man. Leaving the black ox right there without unyoking its arched and probably unbearably aching neck from the weight of the heavy cart that it was dragging, right there in front of the house, old Khúng got down only to feel dizzy. He sensed a black doom hanging over his head but strove not to give in and fall down. As he lumbered up the steep path to his house, the short distance, which was only a few steps away, suddenly appeared too far and difficult to navigate. It felt so hard . . . that he didn't have the strength to carry on. As he approached the house, Lê, his fifth child born after Hương, a dark, sturdy-looking girl came dashing out and hugging the trunk of the mango tree that stood at the end of the alley, started banging her head on a freshly-cut branch crying out to him,

Father, Dũng is dead.

He knew then that for the rest of his life, he would never be able to forget those fateful words. The image of that devastated, helpless, depressed girl, standing with her head resting on the tree-stump, her eyes wide open, announcing her brother's death in that alley, was forever imprinted in his mind. It was also at that exact moment that he suddenly realized that he had to be a pillar of strength for his family at this time of terrible loss. For his wife, first and foremost, and for his children, who were stricken with grief, he was the sole source of strength. He stood still for a moment to gather himself together and after calming his palpitating heart, he gained his composure and walked down the slope with steady steps. He bent down and used all his strength to lift the wheel of the cart, which had toppled when the black ox had collapsed on the ground.

The cart weighed down with stones inched up little by little until it was standing upright. Afterwards, with deliberate steps he entered the house. In the kitchen, his wife, who had passed out, had just regained consciousness. The soldier, who had been a total stranger to the area and had asked neighbours to find old Khúng's house, was now like an old, trusted friend. He was groping around the recesses in the house searching for a kerosene lamp. He found it, lit the lamp and sat leaning on the pillar opposite old Khúng with his backpack held close, covered in dirt and sand that was also scattered on the floor around him. The young soldier began to narrate to both old Khúng and Mrs Huệ how Dũng had sacrificed his life, an incident that he had apparently witnessed in person.

Usually, the people of Thống Nhất—the Unification—village, though they wanted to interact with old Khúng's family, were also wary of doing so. Most of them just wanted to avoid 'crazy old Khúng'. But no one had the heart to dislike or hate him because he was not greedy, malicious, cruel or even sloppy. His only fault was his eccentricity. He was old Khúng . . . uniquely himself and that was the only reason to be vexed with him. In addition, there was another reason. When Mrs Huệ, old Khúng's wife was young, she was a source of distraction for the men in the neighbourhood through no fault of hers. The women in the village were envious of her though no one thought her a slut or a flirt. Where was the sense in flirting with their husbands, who were rough and dirty? It was just that even when Mrs Huệ stood quietly, it was enough to distract the men and dumbfound them.

However, that afternoon, when grief struck that house, if it hadn't been for the neighbours, it would have been difficult for Khúng to manage. This workhorse had always been the calming presence in the family. But on that day, this machine had broken down. So, the neighbours rallied around. Small Choắt's wife joined with some other women to feed the chicken and the pigs, run to the various corners of the garden or house to collect Khúng's children to pat and comfort them.

Old Khúng worked hard to maintain a façade of calmness. It was not until the following morning that he discovered that the previous night, he had forgotten to perform all his routine chores. When he had dismounted from the stone cart to lead the black ox to the stable, he had neglected to fasten the bolt, he had not fed the oxen, which, all night long, had gone hungry without a single blade of grass in his belly.

The soldier from Thanh Hóa, who had been a close friend of Dũng's and other fellow soldiers from the same squad, had buried him in a forest in Northwestern Cambodia bordering Thailand. This had occurred more than six months earlier. The following morning, the soldier took leave, bidding goodbye to both Huệ and Khúng. Two days later, Mrs Huệ was still in no state to get up and function normally. She could not bring herself to eat anything either. But they say that misery seeks company and this is what helped Mrs Huệ. When Mrs Hái, who was over sixty years old and who had numerous progeny, both male and female, and had lost three of her children from the time of the Điện Biện Phủ battle brought over a bowl of porridge, she was able to persuade Mrs Huệ to sit up and drink half a bowl. The next day, Mrs Huệ forced herself to get up, groaning and stumbling, rummaged through the earthen pot, brought it to the well, cleaned it and began to cook a plate of sticky rice to offer for her dead son. For his part, old Khúng cut down a bamboo tree from the bush behind the house with his machete, carried it in, split it in two and wove a mat that was to serve as an altar for their second son, Dũng, on the left side of the room. He then covered the mat with a light green plastic sheet that Nghiên used to cover herself when she went to cut the grass with a sickle. He finally placed a china bowl filled with rice on the altar and looked at his handiwork with satisfaction.

His wife came in from the kitchen and looked at the new altar that had been erected with such care and then gazed at her husband with blank, lifeless eyes. These were no longer the alert eyes of Huệ. They looked more like two dark abysses that had been drained of life. Old Khúng secretly thanked his wife for the way she had conducted herself in the past few days. She had not uttered a word even though he well remembered how, when young Dũng had drunk in the inspirational words that were broadcast and had decided to join the army, she had cried and reprimanded his impulsive, unthinking patriotism. Since his older son, Hùng, was already serving in the army, there was no reason for Dũng to volunteer too. There was no need for him to go. But Mrs Huệ couldn't stop him. She didn't hold onto his hands or legs to prevent him leaving.

It was no wonder that it had taken time and effort for old Khúng to come to terms with the idea that Dũng had sacrificed himself for his Fatherland. The memory of his son's death, when it surfaced, jolted his mind as if it was an ancient bridge across a lake that was constantly in tumult due to its fragility and age. If he let his guard down even for a moment, the deep sadness would surface and he would drop to his feet letting the naked grief envelope him. He would then be filled with fear like a worshipper scared about losing his faith. He had lost his son and there were no utopian visions of his death that safeguarded him from his grief and loss. 'My son', he would mutter to himself, 'I will go to Giát Bridge to get people to magnify your photo, tint it with colour and place it on your altar. That will bring me such fulfillment, joy and honor.' There were many photo shops down at the market. Nor did he lack money. He thought back fondly to the time when Dũng, back then, when he was alive, used to tease his dad for being stingy. But old Khúng had vowed that he would magnify and colour the picture without any thought to the cost as a memorial to the soldier who had died for his country.

He rummaged through old family documents that he had secured inside the hollowed-out tube of a bamboo pole. Inside it, he also found a piece of bait-strap that could be slung over the shoulder. This was a reminder of his occasional fishing expeditions when he went to fish at sea as a young man living in the coastal village of Khơi. Old Khúng then remembered Dũng's backpack, which the soldier from Thanh Hóa had taken the trouble to bring back from Cambodia to give to his family. In the days that followed, Khúng had carefully kept it inside a big container that was used to store sweet potatoes in his wife's room and had completely forgotten about it. Then the old man had run hurriedly into Mrs Huệ's room, had taken out the backpack and had carried it out of the house. Inside it, he was sure that he would discover a photograph of Dũng in his new uniform, where his dignity, good looks and regal bearing would be on display. Old Khúng had felt a profound sadness in his heart. Only after he had taken out the backpack did he have an opportunity to closely scrutinize this extremely precious memento left behind by his dead son. The backpack was so dirty and ragged—it was like a beggar's sack—that he couldn't help but let out a loud cry of woe after which he fell silent as he quietly pulled out the contents one by one. There was nothing there but a few pairs of trousers, an old army shirt that was as tattered and smelly as the backpack, a round metal object that had embossed on it the picture of a Cambodian dancer who appeared to be writhing. He also found a pair of chopsticks that his son hadn't yet evidently finished whittling, made of a strange, unfamiliar wood. The grain was fine and hard as a rock and dark red in colour. Grabbing the bag, he quickly walked out into the alley. As he made his way across the rice fields, he hadn't looked at anyone, and almost didn't notice people, even though they greeted him. He remained silent throughout as he headed straight for the village centre. He had to report his boy's death.

There were two rows of houses that stood parallel to each other like two sides of a ruler. Their doors were wide open. In both, the upper levels were elevated while the lower levels were piled high with harvested peanuts. As he stood outside peering in, he could only see wooden benches and aluminum pots containing the dregs of the green tea that was strewn around. A face as gaunt and withered as a dried bamboo leaf gazed at him from behind the harvested peanuts. Old Khúng had no trouble recognizing Mr Kẹp, Mrs Hái's husband, who was in charge of controlling the traffic of the community and also in ensuring the timely opening and closing of the village centre. Suddenly, on seeing Mr Kẹp, he felt befuddled, confused and bereft of speech. So, Khúng just turned around and walked straight back home. He flung the backpack on the steps, ran into the house and brought out a bottle of white wine and two cups. He filled both cups and using his fingers pushed one to the space before him mumbling,

'Drink, son! In the past, I forbade you though you still drank, slurping it like soup, grinning cheekily, laughing, then choking, talking nonsense to your younger siblings. Your mother was put out and was angry with me for making the drink accessible to you. Yeah . . . but now, she probably won't scold me anymore. And I don't prohibit it anymore. Drink it! Drink as much as you want.'

He appeared drunk. Sitting on the doorstep right in front of the porch, he held in his old, withered hand, his son's chopsticks, both the chopsticks he had been in the middle of whittling in Cambodia as well the ones he had used to eat at home. But here was a pair of chopsticks sharpened with that hard pink wood, its grains almost as hard as stones, fine yet hard, and he thought of that alien country, Cambodia, which was home to this strange tree. That was where this old Khúng's son had fought and fallen. As he sat there, Mrs Hái, his neighbour, came out from the kitchen to see a mourning father sitting with his head bent nearly to his knees, a pair of rosewood chopsticks held slackly in his hands, now falling to the floor. Suddenly, the old man seemed to wake up from a deep sleep and he gazed at the old woman with two blank, bloodshot eyes from which slow tears coursed painfully down his old cheeks.

Mrs Hái sat down next to him and spoke softly to comfort him. 'Dũng has passed on. I know how painful this must be. This is the first time you are navigating this perilous bridge but Mr Kęp and I have negotiated this three times already. We have lost three of our children.' When he heard his neighbour's voice speaking of the tragedy, he rushed to his feet and inching up close to her, he yelled out,

'Yes, but your three children combined were not anywhere as good as this one son of mine.'

'What! How dare you say so . . .!'

3

On the frosty ground, which was as hard as a nutshell, the ox placed its hoofs slowly but surely even though its stride was long.

Suddenly, for no reason, Old Khúng felt a shiver run down his spine as he absorbed the vast night sky that was deep, not lit up with any ground light from the human world below.

Yes, the black ox was heading to the market to be slain but he was also heading to his death, after all! He knew his final destiny but did this animal know it? He must sense it, thought old Khúng. Spending the hardest part of his life in the forest with this animal for company, old Khúng was still not sure if his animal friend was smart or stupid. Humans had an adage which went, 'as stupid as an ox', but he wondered if this were indeed true. He had noticed through the course of his life that there were occasions when it seemed that his companion had sensed and understood some things more quickly than he had. But perhaps, in general, it *was* stupid? But if it was indeed inherently dull, uncomprehending and blameless, the old man felt he only loved it more because of these qualities. His ox felt to him like a child who had never grown up despite its massive body. Now, he felt the cart shaking violently. What was happening? He had been curled up in a corner in his worn-out chestnut-coloured coat that had not quite warmed him. Now, as he sat up, he suddenly saw a star falling at the edge of the sky. In fact, he had not seen that star before its fall nor did he register its demise but only caught it during that moment of falling. Suddenly, at the western edge of the horizon there appeared to be sparks of fire that were tinged with gold. Then, as he looked on, they quickly disappeared. He tried searching for the sparks again but there was no sign of them. Was that not a sign that someone had just died?

Was there someone, somewhere, in this vast and endless earth who had just died or was about to? The star that had just fallen may not be a harbinger of death for the

ox since the divine Nam Tào and Bắc Đẩu, who decided
the destiny of humans, would surely not have enough free
time to signal the deaths of even animals? No star would
have fallen to signal the impending death of the black ox, no
matter how hard and with how much sand and dirt, it had
worked. Or was this star his son's? Was it a path to heaven
that was paved by the hero who had saved his country . . .
of Dũng himself, who had held a gun bravely to fight in
the Cambodian war? But surely that couldn't be since in
fact, Dũng had been dead for more than a year and a half?
Has it been that long? Or, was it a messenger from heaven
foretelling his own death?

Suddenly, he felt nervous. Inside his loose tunic he felt
his shoulders and back tightening with anxiety. He recalled
how, for some time now, he had had a persistent cough and
ache in his bones. He would also often get nightmares where
he saw the dead. Also, he had of late been very forgetful
and confused. Sometimes he would forget that he had
already eaten and at other times, when it was not yet quite
dawn, he would think it was already day and would urge
his sleeping daughter to wake up and go to work causing a
lot of confusion in the house. As his mind paced back and
forth restlessly, old man Khúng gradually felt calm descend
on him. He gathered himself and thought, *How would
someone ordinary like him, a lifelong farmer who spent his
days walking behind a cow, merit a falling star in the sky?*
That would not happen in a very long time . . . *only in Tet
time*, he thought cynically.

As he sat and groaned with his aches and pains in
the cart, old Khúng, all of a sudden, felt embarrassed and
ashamed because he felt he had briefly been puffed up with

his own self-importance, like the time when Mr Bời had forced him to become the Chair of the Youth Union in the Farmer's Congress. He clicked his tongue impatiently. What was wrong with him? He didn't need any celestial body, neither the moon nor the stars, nor indeed even the sun. All he needed was the ground beneath his feet and his small, family-owned, cultivated, field.

Yet, old Khúng couldn't help gazing up at the sky, his eyes scouring the four corners with a curiosity that was both paradoxically skeptical and respectful. He took careful note of a few bright blue stars, the biggest and the brightest, and believed them to be the ones that spoke of the destiny of kings and rulers. Alas, what a lot of stars filled the night sky! The more he looked, the more stars came into view. While beneath their starry firmament, it appeared at this moment that there was only the ox and the old man plodding on in the vast, dark ground of the earth.

As he sat gazing at the sky, facing the dense darkness ahead and the chill of the cold night wind, Khúng suddenly let out an involuntary chuckle causing the walking ox to halt. The old man didn't use a knife to prod the animal to move but used his hand to pat the animal on its flank.

'Go, Go! Nothing has happened!' He continued to chuckle while talking to his animal companion. 'Go on! I'm not laughing at you. Ha ha! I daren't laugh at you. I'm only laughing at the stars in the sky.'

All the leaders and celebrities of the present day! All alive with a star to their names. They believed they were illuminating the earth and that, without them, the earth would turn dark, like a tightly closed jar; that without their illuminating presence, thousands, millions of people, would open their eyes to be confronted by darkness, not able to see their way forward. But it was all so futile. God knew how many stars there were in the sky. Surely billions, which were blinking, sweating, heaving to push out light, like a woman panting to give birth to a baby. The whole sky was littered with stars and yet beneath them, the ground was still dark like this and the way to Giát market was sheathed in pitch darkness like a tightly closed jar.

That was what made it so ludicrous. Both he and his old ox had walked a lot that night but they had never got lost. It was not just his pathway that was dark but his head was filled with equally dense thoughts. The only saving grace was that like a night owl's, God had given him two eyes that could penetrate the darkness. Old Khúng, a farmer all his life, walked steadily behind the old ox as it cut furrows in the dark road . . .

He turned again to look at the falling star as it fell to its demise like the flickering ash at the tip of a cigarette butt. He wondered if maybe this was just a small star, of modest size, or perhaps it was the star of the famous district party secretary, who had recently retired from his position. Indeed, it was possible to believe that, sadly, there was a new law in the universe which decreed that if the person no longer held power, it made no difference if he was dead or alive; the star would die along with his power. To be honest, until this moment, old Khúng was not sure whether he loved or hated, liked or disliked, the most powerful man in the district, Mr Bởi. He was familiar with the powerful General Secretary of the Party but, equally, he was a sincere friend to old Khúng.

But old Khúng himself, although he recognized how friendly and egalitarian Mr Bởi was, felt happier keeping his distance from people in power. He did, however, reserve a space in his heart to admire such people. Though he may have had his doubts about them or recognized their inner contradictions, he still had to admire them.

Mr Bởi had originally been a cow trader and indeed a farmer through and through from the tip of his hair to his heels, like old Khúng. But he was never disturbed by the mundane like old Khúng. Mr Bởi was always caught up in grand things that needed the use of hundreds of thousands of people to work hard with fan flags displayed in the sky. He loved crowds and liked to be bustling around all the time. He wasted a lot of human energy and caused a lot of damage ... but he could do something well. It was there for all to see.

Lao Khúng thought, *It is going to be difficult to find a replacement for old Bởi.* He was not greedy. It was no easy task for everyone to understand farmers and to take advantage of their mentality. But Bởi was good, a leader who dared to think, dared to take action, dared to take on responsibilities; he was always thinking, always walking, forever talking, perpetually pointing out things that needed to be done, andalways planning, great, great things. Old Khúng thought respectfully of old Bởi. He was a man who, regardless of whether he was talented or ignorant in his work, would still stir things up—either the hunger or the satisfaction of thousands of people for many years to come.

How terrible it had been, when he had carried out the great mechanization of agriculture in the whole district.

He deleted the names of the villages: three communes merged into one factory while temples and shrines were removed. Also, no one knew from where he had procured so many machines. They were crawling on the road like crabs. The oxen and cows were afraid that they had become unemployed! The radical revolutionary of the time was always like a cauldron of boiling water. He always speeded ahead doing whatever he wanted to do regardless of the consequences of his actions. His goal was to turn the world upside down.

The district leader, Mr Bời, came from the same class as old Khúng. Therefore, he always aimed all his revolutionary activity (*cái cách mạng*)[35] at the rural poor, the subalterns. During those years, Mr Bời's prestige skyrocketed, and everyone was afraid of him since he appeared to be the man of choice, who carried out all the plans to spread socialism in the countryside implementing government policies.

From the time he was humble and poor, to when he served as the chairman of the district, Mr Bời had been firm friends with old Khúng.

Old Khúng had found it very odd that the chairperson of the district sought out his company. He drove over and invited Khúng to hang out with him and on these trips forced Khúng to argue with him about some random topic. This was not difficult for Khúng, of course, for he was not afraid and argued fiercely with the district chair. Both their faces would turn red with emotion and they would be foaming at the mouth but still they would be matched so equally, it

---

[35] 'cái cách mạng' is from the Vietnamese translation of *Ah Q* by Lu xun [this foonote is in the original Vietnamese text].

would be hard to decide who had won the argument and who had lost. But later, when he became the Party General Secretary, the chairman did not indulge in that foolish game anymore. What man in power would want to have someone continually argue and disagree with him?

In fact, even the very first time this happened, old Khúng had been smart enough to figure out the true situation. So, he only pretended to argue, not divulging his true thoughts to the district chairman. That was probably the reason why the friendship between the chairman and Khúng remained intact. However, old Khúng believed that those were the times when Mr Bời was more likable because people were not intimidated by his power. Back then, Mr Bời was quite attached to the black ox for he still knew how to love cattle and animals. As he gently dozed, seated in the cart, old Khúng recalled the new years when peace had reigned with the US. The whole district was being gathered in sand trucks to build the Quỳnh Thuận salt flats with the help of buffaloes and oxen to stave off hunger for thousands of coastal people. The whole district had gathered there— Mr Bời called it the 'great gathering' in order to make it appear a powerful movement. At that time, Dũng was still only a child, a naughty child in the neighbourhood. The ox had still looked young, fit, and sturdy.

From the day he was born, Dũng and the ox lived out a socialist fantasy. A hand-crafted building site (*công trường*) similar to the names mentioned in some books by Karl Marx. It was Chairman Bời who had made this fantasy a reality. In every corner of the district, men, women, the elderly and the children were harnessed in the thousands to work in the salt-flats. Also, more buffaloes and oxen were put to work. Before they entered the district, the people of the communes and their cattle were organized into several cadres: battalions, regiments, divisions with commanders and political commissars, advancing troops with trumpets, retreating troops with trumpets, female drummers, frog drummers, cadres with bunting flags, banana leaf flags, god procession flags, red flags with yellow stars, troops with gaudy cloth and paper badges stapled on their shoulders and sleeves. Every session had loudspeakers and it resounded with announcements every hour when the whole site was informed about the productivity and its advancements.

After three weeks of being immersed in the atmosphere of the great construction site, old Khúng, his son and the ox were able to return home. All three returned to the yoke field where they ran into the district president's jeep which was driving uphill.

Mr Bời drove past in a jeep and looked back. He spied a bony, sinewy old man jumping down from the ox cart and loudly scolding the boy seated in front of the cart. Chairman Bời, bellowed out, 'Hi!' He immediately recognized the animal that was pulling the cart gracefully, like a dancer. He recognized it to be the rebellious black ox that had caused a commotion in the salt fields. The district president ordered the driver to halt his car in the middle of the road. Originally a cattle-trader, he had a connoisseur's eye. He walked close to the black ox and appraised it with the passion of a trader. He was completely taken up by the merits of the black ox and couldn't help but utter words of praise. Indeed, the blood of the cattle-trader that ran through his veins appeared to have revived because he went a few more rounds surveying the ox closely. The more he scrutinized the animal, the more satisfied he appeared to be. It seemed he couldn't bring himself to fault a single feature. At last he sighed and said, 'Oh my! An ox as beautiful as *Xi Shi*.'[36]. He then turned to look at the cart owner.

Right then, old Khúng was annoyed because he had lost the cart-spring that was used as suspension. Though Khúng stopped scolding Dũng for being careless enough to lose it, he still felt deeply unhappy that he had lost his property, almost as if one of his vital organs had been cut out. He felt as though he had been kicked hard by a cow. He felt doubly upset since both his son and he had neglected to take off the suspension. So, as though to add salt to the wound, he had to go to the capital, Hanoi, to procure the suspension that was needed.

The whole of his uncle's family that lived there had to use all their network and connections to find all the different parts that were needed for the cart: the ball-bearings, axle, tires. He had been robbed of valuable steel parts. *When will I be able to buy these again?* Sometimes, even with money one couldn't buy these parts. So, now, from morning onwards, from the moment he left to the moment he rode back home, each time he went over a steep bumpy road, he jumped down, doubling his butt to the skies and scolded his son even as he peered at the gap left below the floor of the cart—a space left by the thieves as a souvenir for him; the place left bare when the cart's suspension was stolen. He cursed the thieves heartily!

---

[36] One of the renowned Four Beauties of ancient China.

But now, when he noticed that the district president couldn't resist stopping his car to eye his beautiful black ox, his heartache at the loss of his property was somewhat relieved.

Slowly mounting the last slope, old Khúng and the president walked side by side of the cart, each trying to demonstrate to the other through their comments about the ox, how knowledgeable they were about the animal's worthy qualities.

However, when the district president moved on to enquire about his impressions of the past few days of bustle, working on the socialist project, old Khung's heartache at having lost his cart parts, burst forth as anger.

'I don't see the point of the socialist construction project! They are a bunch of thieves', Khung retorted angrily.

The district chairman was offended. His face turned red but he still tried to restrain his speech.

'What's wrong? Is anything the matter, old man?' he enquired.

But old Khung wasn't mollified. 'They're all a bunch of thieves. They stole a whole set of the cart's suspension parts from me.' The old man scowled even more. 'They are all robbers, these dreadful people at the construction site.'

President Bởi was furious. He couldn't hear any criticism about his construction project.

'How dare you criticize this important "party project"?' he scolded.

'Sir, when my property gets stolen, I have every right to complain and declare that it was stolen. This obviously happened last night, right there at the construction site . . .'

'Are you sure?'

'Do you really think that at my age, I would say that I lost something, if I hadn't? Khúng asked irately.

'Yes, I know that you won't. By the way, which commune are you from?'

'Hùng Tráng.'

'And, what is your name?'

'May I know why you want to know it?'

'. . . .'

'Oh well, my name is old Khúng, everyone knows.'

The district president rolled his eyes.

'You . . . Ha! Are you the old Khúng from Hùng Tráng commune?'

'That's right.'

'Ah! Let this district president shake hands with Mr Khúng.'

Mr Bởi's face was sweaty and his boots were impatiently stomping on the pavement. But he looked at the interlocutor curiously and respectfully as though he was looking at a man who had successfully opened mountains and had found earth from the dawn of time and had just returned to stand in front of him.

Two months later, when it was the plowing season in Hùng Tráng, the most difficult period of year for both cattle and humans, Mr Bởi drove his car straight to Mr Khúng's house declaring his intention of staying a week in the old man's house to learn how to do business and live and work together with the others in the neighbourhood. Initially, old Khúng didn't believe him, and his family members were petrified and anxious. They were convinced that Khúng had committed some grave error, so terrible that the district chairman had to personally come and investigate it.

Mrs Huệ hastily smuggled out her stock of 'pig bubbles'—a part of the pig's intestines in which she had cached smuggled wine—that she had hidden at the bottom of jars in her room, to her neighbours' house to hide it there.

For the first meal, Mrs Huệ chased a hen into the kitchen, grabbed its legs and was about to slay it but Mr Khúng stopped her. 'We serve our guest no more or no less than what we eat. That's the way it goes', he said firmly. He explained the meaning of the guest's work to his wife. However, no sooner had Mrs Huệ dutifully released the hen that Mr Khúng grabbed it and suggested that she actually slay the chicken after all, since, well, 'Who doesn't like delicious food?' Well, we don't quite know what the purpose of his stay in my house is, so, let's give him a delicious chicken meal first. This is, after all, the district chairman, not an ordinary man. Perhaps he has come here to make himself famous. Who knows? Our house may become famous too.' *Sometimes, life can uncover strange things*, old Khúng thought and smiled to himself.

So, for a whole week, all activities in old Khúng's family had been turned upside down. Khúng's son, Bút, then less than five years old, just learning to walk in the open beach, was rather shy, huddled in the kitchen with his mother or hiding all day, his eyes wide open, gazing at the stranger in the house with hostility and suspicion. Though both old Khúng and his wife tried to act normally, trying to maintain an easy atmosphere, the whole neighbourhood was uneasy and kept prying on this tiled house with a lime tree in its front alley, where a strange event was taking place: the district president, no less, was not sitting in a jeep to raise his hands to wave at the people who were plowing and hoeing on both sides of the road. Nor did he give long speeches standing on the wooden platform erected in front of the district Hall; nor did he enjoy himself eating and drinking at parties. Instead, he actually rolled up his pants all the way up, and together with Khúng and his son, worked hard from morning until night. What was more, he still appeared to want only simple meals. When Mrs Huệ served food on a wooden tray with two bowls and two pairs of chopsticks for her husband and the guest to eat separately from the rest of the family, the chairman would have none of it. He immediately came down to the kitchen and picked up a chair to sit on. He would sit in a corner of the bamboo ditch, mingle freely with the rest of the children in his host's crowded house. He would eat the bowls of sliced sweet potato stuck with a few grains of rice as decoration.

This actually upset old Khúng and his wife. It was as if they were witnessing their lives through the eyes of this nobleman peering with knowing eyes into the bottom of their rice bowl and his hand reaching into their daily lives. Although the stranger was no thief, it still felt as if he had stolen their privacy. Like everyone else living in poverty, old Khúng and his wife were not keen for outsiders to know the extent of their indigent circumstances—neither their needs, the poverty, their lack and their meager portions, nor indeed their flip side—their meagre affluence. In short, all the many ways that they managed to hold life and soul together like every other household in their neighbourhood.

All these private feelings, however, they kept to themselves and Mr Bời was no wiser. He was actually very pleased with himself. He knew that sooner or later the fact of his staying in old Khung's house would spread throughout the district, indeed throughout the province, and his actions would be the talk of the cadres and ordinary people.

He felt he had done right to choose to live in old Khúng's house among all the houses in the district because this was the last stronghold of individual business. No one could decide whether he was in earnest or if he was just fooling around. But his aim was to turn old Khúng into a new socialist member. The chairman entrusted this job to himself almost like a religious acolyte who had volunteered to convert someone into a believer, in what was an arduous and dangerous mission. The district chairman took advantage of every possible circumstance to lure old Khúng into arguing with him about the 'two-way' theory *(hai con đường)*. Old Khúng listened to the chairman's words with every appearance of due reverence and in silence, trying to curb his tongue so that he wouldn't burst out with any foolhardy sentiments such as, 'I have ten children, if we went into the cooperative group, we would surely starve to death'—words which were actually hovering on his lips.

It must be noted that in that momentous week, out of all the members of the Khúng family, the black ox was the only one who was able to interact with the guest in a dispassionate and forthright manner though one could say that a distinct dearth of the spirit of politeness and due respect for the guest were noticeable. Never once did Mr Bời place a yoke on the ox's hump; what is more, it once kicked the district chairman with his cheerful, open, fat, round face in the middle of his stomach leading to him falling headlong in the fields.

Suddenly old Khúng addressed the ox loudly so that it could hear him despite walking ahead of the cart, 'Do you remember that time when I had to rush over and raise my hands to lift the district chairman up and then pick up the plow whip, which had dropped out of his hand. I had to beat you hard then. As there is a god above you witnessing my words to you, I can assert that living with you and working together for a lifetime, I have never had the heart to ever whip you. Your flesh and skin is my flesh and skin. It's true. If you hurt, then I hurt too. However, at that time, when the district chairman was lying there holding his stomach and writhing in pain, right in the middle of the field, I had no choice but to turn the whip to beat you with all my strength. Also, while my hand beat, my mouth cursed you using all the curse words in the language. Moreover, when you kicked the president causing him to fall, the boy Dũng, who was standing at the edge of the field, had the cheek to grin and laugh out loud, filled with glee. That meant that I had to hit you doubly hard to make up for his impudence. Was he stupid or what? Perhaps it was just his youthfulness that led him to behave so inappropriately. One knows that at times like these, even if you're laughing inside until you feel your stomach will burst, you should know to keep your face straight and not reveal your mirth. You don't ever laugh at your superiors. That man was the president of the district.' Well! Even before his death, had his son been any wiser? But Dũng had inherited his straightforward temperament from his father. Old Khúng had passed it on to him through his genes. But where was he now, that carefree boy Dũng? In which world was he wandering?

4

As daylight came, old Khúng fell asleep in the cart. The dew drops fell as fat as grains of corn, clattering on the hooves of the black ox causing the cold to creep under its feet and pushing it to walk faster.

The coastal line was covered in white mist. Weaving between the mist, at times, it was as though a row of glittering beads glimmered for a while before they disappeared. These were the headlights of the trucks plying down Street One in convoys, just entering the bend at the beginning of Cầu Giát Street. He was on the hilly 'cow-rolling slope' (*Dốc bò lăn*). His ox and he were crossing a road that ran past fields, which had been newly plowed the previous afternoon. The ox opened his nostrils and inhaled contentedly. Only it could fully savour all the flavours emanating from the freshly plowed soil that radiated from the fields on both sides of the road.

Initially, the old man was trying to fight off his sleep that was trying to shut down his mind, which had been groping dark places. Also, due to his old back pain, he was leaning on the bundles of firewood and felt more comfortable. He even thought, this time the wife has sent Hương, his daughter, only slim barks of firewood. It would be difficult for her to sell them. She would have to make several trips to the market to sell all of them. He leant over to pull the cloth bag that was filled with dried sweet potato mixed with rice. Hương, his daughter in her school, would have to survive on this meal for half a month. Even as his hand was tugging at the bag, his head rested on it and it felt so soft.

No emperor sleeping on his luxurious bed in the palace could be this happy, he thought humorously, as he crossed his arms over his stomach tugging at the lapels of his dung-coloured coat to hug it tight. Let the black ox be! No need to worry about it now! After that affectionate thought which brought him happiness, his mind went completely blank and it was not under his control any longer. He tucked his head to one side, let his arms go lax, made himself comfortable and began snoring with that deliciously familiar rhythm that he adopted every night at home.

The black ox knew that Khúng was asleep though it didn't turn to look. It calmly pulled the cart up and down the undulating landscape. Even if old Khúng chose to sleep until late in the day, the ox would have been able to carry both the cart and him down to Cầu Giát Street, to the dormitory of high school students who stayed in the hostel at the other side of the cement bridge. It had taken that road many times to Giát market. A beam of light shone on the ox from behind as a truck sped past. The vehicle carefully edged close to the side of the road, almost coming to a halt near the cart before slowly edging forward. The bright beam of the headlights from behind and the rumble of the motor near him still did not wake up the old man but it caught him in the midst of a deep sleep and in the coils of a terrible dream, a version of which he had previously had at home.

He dreamed again but unlike the previous time, he found that it was he who was beaten with a sledgehammer! Indeed, it was he who was the ox! He surveyed himself in his half-ox, half-human body, drenched in blood and yet he remained as calm as though this were his natural aspect, a fact that he had not quite assimilated in his waking state.

Still in that same bizarre shape, he was walking with Secretary Bời on a flat strip of land on a warm plateau in the highlands. Both old Bời and Khúng with his strange body were following Lạc, Khúng's son, who was going to reclaim land in Dak Lak. The three of them stumbled as they walked like people walking on stilts on a land that appeared to hang from the middle of the sky. As they walked on, they couldn't find a single drop of water anywhere the whole day. The soil beneath the old man's feet appeared to be fertile, not red like lacquer, freshly plowed, the soil broken up by a tractor, and each pink powdery grain of soil was flying around rhythmically like flowing water beside the lush forests. The leaves, blue like in a painting, were rustling.

In the dream, as night fell, the darkness was drenched in magic and the ox, now incarnated as half-ox and half-man suddenly became exhilarated, ecstatic as it inhaled the smell and texture of the plowed earth. Now it was standing all alone in the middle of the Dak Lak plateau, which had only been plowed by the new settlers. It saw that in a short while it would be morning and it would need to leave the furrows to return to live in the countryside in the green forest. This half-ox-man was a wild animal or rather a domestic animal that had rediscovered its wildness. It had found its way back to an eternally free life.

By now, old Khúng was well and truly awake. Though he inhabited his normal everyday body, his emotions were still obsessive like those of the ox that had preoccupied him in the dream, its residual effect still having a hold over him. He stretched his limbs out, touching each bicep and calf methodically, one by one, as though taking stock, and was relieved to find that he was still an intact human being.

Continuing to lie with his head on the bag of dried sweet potatoes and rice that he was taking to deliver to his daughter, carefully calibrated to carry her through at least half a month, he once again rubbed his hands and feet and touched his bottom to ensure that he hadn't sprouted a tail. Only when he felt completely reassured that there was truly nothing to worry about did he stop. But the old man's eyes did not stray from the ox with its four sturdy legs as it ceaselessly covered the distance ahead with grinding monotony. Khúng felt a great affinity, as he had in the true form that he had only once experienced.

After he had smoked a cheroot (*thuốc lào*) he felt completely awake again, and the more alert he became, the more he was given to reflection. The confused link that had established itself between the ox and himself would not leave him. He recalled the forest of his dream with its dark green leaves, the tall *Erythrophleum Fordii* and the pine trees growing on the slopes of the cliffs, the wild oxen walking precariously on the rocky cliffs or peacefully grazing in the bright, sunny forests. In the midst of the herd of oxen he saw his own face, the most relaxed and serene there. If he were to narrate his thoughts to someone, they would mock him. Suddenly, old Khúng decided on a crazy course of action. He decided that he would set his ox free. The conviction came upon him that his previously decided course of action was inhumane. All his life, the ox had been pulling the plow to support his family. But he was repaying the animal's devotion by selling it to butchers to slaughter it! He had come to the realization that he was part of the animal. He was no longer exclusively human. He didn't feel the need to condemn and abuse himself. He only felt an urgent need to free himself. At that moment, the ox was pulling the cart through a patch of sparsely wooded forest.

'Stop! Stop!'

Old Khúng called out to his animal-helper in a slightly raised voice. The ox obediently came to a halt. It appeared surprised. Khúng jumped down, went to the side of the ox, and putting both hands on its sturdy neck, which was damp with dew and sweat, patted the animal affectionately before unyoking it and placing the yoke beside its front legs. The animal raised its neck, and sticking its neck out, licked its master's shoulders and neck. Everytime the fleshy but rough tongue touched his flesh, old Khúng felt goosebumps on his skin. He felt as though the ox could sense his thoughts and had reached its conclusions, 'He was untying it forever!'

Old Khúng suddenly felt the need to hurry. He pulled the cart to the side of the road and hid it behind the dusty rocks and foliage and returned to the animal that remained standing where it had before. 'I'm setting you free now,' he whispered to his beloved animal in a slightly gruff voice. 'I think that you have served me long enough, son, now go! Go to the forest to live the rest of your life. There's plenty of grass in the forest. You can eat as much as you want for the rest of your life. If you are thirsty, you can drink spring water. You can choose to live either alone or with a herd of wild oxen. They are all happy and free like kings and queens wandering these mountains, never having to pull a plow or a cart . . .Go, go! Come on! Get going!' He wound the rope that he had removed from the black ox's snout with his hands. He then hit it forcefully on the side, forcing it to run into the woods. The only way to free the ox was by exiling him to the forest never to be seen again. As the ox walked away, old Khúng stood there holding his whip ready to smack his ass until it hurt to prevent him from stopping or looking back.

This strange chase went on quietly through the long dark pre-dawn hours. The more he urged the animal to run into the forest, the further it was from the 'cow-rolling' road. That made old Khúng feel more secure. He felt a quiet peace and self-satisfaction steal over him. Was it because he could feel the sordid fate that had been decided for him— for the half-human animal—had now been banished? The farther up the forest it went, the more dense the forest would become. The trunks of the perennial spice tree, the *dổi* tree,[37] were covered with thick foliage.

Once you passed a few streams on the way, you entered a dense forest that grew on the rocky mountains. This forest was darker and this was the mountainous area where wild oxen wandered about. The oxen that had served as cattle remembered the taste of salt in the hot summer months. At night, they sometimes visited Kinh (ethnic Vietnamese) families, wandered into the kitchen and licked briefly the iron bars of the stove or *ông đầu rau* (the head of the kitchen god). Sometimes, at midnight when there was a bright moon, the young calves got together in groups of five or seven to destroy the crops in the fields of the locals on the opposite side of the mountain. People had tried stalking, organizing ambushes, or digging trenches to plant poles to trap them. However, they had still not managed to catch a single one of them. These wild oxen were so canny!

---

[37] A spice tree growing mostly in Northwest Vietnam.

The task of driving the black ox deeper into the forest lasted for hours. Old Khúng was tired but refused to stop. He was determined that it must go far, as deep into the forest as possible, so that there was no way back to the old man. Then, when he returned home tomorrow, he decided he would tell the truth to Mrs Huệ, that he hadn't taken the ox to Giát market to sell but instead on the way, he had set it free and given it back its life by chasing it into the forest to join a herd of wild oxen. He was sure that Huệ would understand and not get upset with him. She would, in fact, sympathize with him for his decision. After he had driven the animal far into the other side of the rugged mountainside, old Khúng tenderly bid farewell to his helpmate by turning the head of the whip, beating the ox with all his strength, cursing it with his mouth, and again, beating it with his hand. As it writhed in pain and nearly collapsed on its four legs, the old man abruptly turned his back on it and without saying another word, he left, disappearing into the darkness. When he returned to the cart, the predawn darkness had given way to early dawn. He knew that from here on, what was left was only a third of the dirt road and that the roads would be far better. He looked at the bundles of firewood and the pile of green tea on the roof of the cart, took the time to puff another cheroot, and then, alone, he pulled the cart to the middle of the road and continued the downhill journey.

The sweaty smell of the ox that had survived several arduous journeys wafted through the wooden yoke and mingled with his own salty sweat. Above his head, as the light chased away the darkness, he could still spot a few scattered stars that were turning blurry as if they were about to fall off the sky or disappear. The old man pulled the wheeled cart in-between the row of other carts pulled by buffaloes or oxen, which were steadily overtaking him. Sometimes a convoy of trucks carrying coal or logs passed by carrying their goods to Giát market with a loud clattering sound. Finally, at about seven o'clock in the morning, old Khúng was able to drag the cart to the entrance of the Giát Bridge district. But that time there was hardly enough space to even walk on Highway Street One.

Old Khúng took off the yoke from his shoulder and sat down cross-legged wearily on the grass beside the cobbled road that had been trodden by oxen for such a long time. The old man raised his head to peer at the road that cut through Highway One leading straight down to the sea. That was the only way for him to go back to the village. At night the gravel shone brightly. He rested for half an hour. Then, after smoking two pine cheroots, he sat contentedly. Though very tired, he still felt very happy as though he had accomplished a great task that he had always dreamed of but had had no way of fulfilling. This human now seemed to have split in two, one half of him living the life of the black ox grazing in the forest on the mountainside, while the other half lived the life of an old farmer, struggling alone with the cart in the middle of the road.

Cầu Giát Street, that well-known, bustling district, was waking up to the hustle and bustle of the market day. That section of Highway Street One that ran through Cầu Giát Street was nearly two kilometres long on both sides of the bridge. One side of this road was already filled with the smell of water fish and the odor of fresh fish while the other side of the road was filled with the stench of cow dung. The strident movement of every ox, buffalo, cow, calves pulling carts, and calves that moved along in single file, could be felt on the road. They were all pouring into the market. The herd of animals was growing larger by the minute as they packed the entire road. People looking up from the forest uphill and those gazing up from the sea below, would have all been able to see this sight of people and cattle endlessly moving along in groups and herds. Laughter and arguments accompanied the people, as well as the sound of wooden wheels scratching the road, hot and heavy. The noise of the heavy poles being carried and the cows mooing, the hiss of whips as they whistled through the air and their lashing of the hips of the animals pulling the carts, reverberated and filled the air. In the midst of all this, when a truck or a vehicle rushed past, it made the people scream.

The most assertive of everyone there, however, and that included the animals and the trucks, were the fisherfolk, the women from the coastal fishing villages who were so pushy. They moved in groups of five to ten; tall, sturdy women, their skirts swinging around their knees, with ragged bras, semi-naked almost, sweating profusely. They shouted as they ran backwards and forwards in order to clear the roads to sell their fish. Their other weapon of attack and self-defence were their elbows that they used like clubs to shove people.

Old Khúng painstakingly avoided these fisherwomen, who were vending their fish in a frenzied manner. He was wary that in their crazed selling, these 'willows and delicate peaches' might accidentally knock over his cart loaded with firewood and green tea. Since he was the sole-puller of the cart, trying to manoeuver his way to the other side of the bridge, he had no other recourse but to follow a lorry that was loaded with pigs and hence moved forward slowly like a bartender balancing many glasses. At least this ensured that the firewood and the tea loaded in the cart was safe and that Khúng wasn't as tired. Already, he was quite exhausted. As he got closer to the market gate, the crowds were heaving and the animals were thronging and there was hardly space to stand. The old man wiped the sweat from his face with his sleeve, and when his eyes cleared, he looked around him to the sides and in front and behind him, and all he could see was a sea of gray humanity filled with endless cattle, with people driving them to the market to sell them for meat. As he walked, old Khúng encountered something that troubled him and pushed him towards self-reflection. He found himself looking deeply into the eyes of an ox that was wearily walking alongside him with slow, dragging steps. It was a bull that was almost completely without hair and appeared to have lived for a few decades. Its jaw was sagging as if the bones had melted away through the years. Its two large, sunken eyes gazed at him—the silent, resigned and patient eyes of an old animal that was calmly walking towards its death.

Old Khúng managed to pull his cart out of the way of the long line of all the old cows that were being driven along to the market to be sold for meat.

All of a sudden, he heard someone hailing him. 'Hi, Mr Khúng! I'd like to invite you to come right in and share a bowl of beef stew and curry with me.'

Old Khúng, who had just pulled his cart to the side of the road looked up to see who it was. He saw behind the trees, a row of beef stalls with red meat hanging in front. The man who had called out to him was even then slicing meat. In-between, even as he greeted Khúng, the old butcher made time to furtively reach out and pinch his young and beautiful wife standing beside him.

'Come in and share a bowl of fresh beef with curry sauce and bread, Mr Khúng! Where did your ox go that you have to bend your back to pull the cart like this?' he asked.

The owner of the *phở* shop was an old friend of Khúng's. But he didn't want to stop now. He hastily pulled his cart away from the shop. However, wherever he turned, in every street, he only saw the horrible sight of the red meat hanging from rows of iron hooks. Traders, drivers, officials on business trips, and visitors from the north or south of the country were making the most of the opportunity to buy fresh beef from this market located right on Highway One. This busy market town had an unending supply of meat from oxen and cattle. The local entrepreneurs were devising ways to pool their capital and buy vehicles with refrigeration units so that they could more easily transport the abundant beef available here to Hanoi and other cities where there was always a scarce supply of beef for restaurants.

Like a man fleeing a brutal massacre, old Khúng hastily pulled his cart to the other side of the bridge. But there was no escaping the oxen plodding along the road. Now, he viewed them as bloody, walking corpses ready to be killed for meat rather than as live animals pulling carts.

He turned into a crooked tar road, past a tranquil church and then walked into a building that appeared to be an abandoned cooperative warehouse with broken brick walls. This was the high school building where his daughter was attending as a twelfth grade student. The solemn atmosphere of the school where classes were being conducted washed over him like a balm, enabling him to regain a measure of calm. Khúng pulled the cart around the back of the school, past the fields and finally came to a halt in front of the boarding house of students whose families lived far away. The hostel was nothing more than a few rows of ruined, thatched cottages resembling structures in a conscripted labour camp.

Old Khúng headed straight to a familiar room at the end of the row, which his daughter shared with a few of her classmates. The door was locked. He was about to unload the firewood and other items from the cart to leave them in front of his daughter's room, when suddenly, his attention was caught by the sight of his old black ox munching steadily on grass beside the girls' volleyball court next door. As he laid eyes on this old, familiar face, he was dumbfounded. The black one that he had personally and determinedly driven into the forest in the dark pre-dawn hours had found its way here. He had deliberately used the whip mercilessly beating it hard to drive it towards a free life but to no avail.

The ox looked up at the old man with eyes that looked sorrowful and filled with longing. It was the look of a creature that had returned willingly, accepting its fate. Standing silently next to his loaded cart, which he had toiled to pull all the way, Khúng didn't know how to react to the animal's presence. He couldn't bring himself to blame the animal, so he just gazed at this old friend, his close business partner, with eyes that were filled with deep sadness.

Translated from *Tuyển Tập Truyện Ngắn Hay Nhất Của Nguyễn Minh Châu*. Hà Nội: Nhà xuất bản văn học, 2022.

Tiger Smell (1987)

Quý Thể (1940)

'Honey!' she called out softly to me.

I pretended to be asleep.

We were angry at each other. I knew last night she had come home at around midnight. She had taken off her glittery costume and hung it on a hook. She had then entered the bathroom and I heard the sound of her stepping into the 'lotus-shower'. Then, I heard the bathroom door open. She slowly climbed into the bed beside me.

I have heard her going through these rituals day in and day out. However, though we had been quarrelling for over a week now, I still didn't think it was the time for a reconciliation.

'Why are you in bed so early?' She whispered and gently touched my shoulder. It felt like an invitation. 'Honey, I've just finished my bath'. She followed up on her words by embracing me and whispering softly, 'Let me give you a surprise tonight.'

She hugged me and her body felt cool and slightly damp after her bath. A new and delightful scent that emanated from her body assailed my senses . . . the scent of roses. I had never known her to use this perfume before. I woke up completely now. I saw her again as the soft, gentle, and special girl I had first met and got to know, who had exuded a seductive scent that had always awakened all my senses. She had turned into a completely new woman for me tonight, and perhaps for her as well. I detected in all her gentle gestures a secret joy. The past few days of acrimony appeared to have disappeared.

This is how the healing process begins . . . always. She is the one who appears reasonable and I invariably come across as the obstinate spouse. This was her holding out the olive branch after us having been mad at each other for a whole week. The issue at hand is quite straightforward:

I have repeatedly asked her to quit her job but she refuses.

I am a math professor at a prestigious local university. She is an actress and an animal trainer. She specializes in training and performing with tigers in a circus. However, if you need to compare notes on our professional success, I can confirm that she is far more famous than I am. Her income, too, is more than mine. But I find her exotic profession off-putting though she has always claimed to love tigers.

'They love me and I love my job. What else can I do? Be a secretary or a saleswoman? It's not easy to find a job in these professions. Also, it is fairly easy to train to become a secretary. It requires arduous training to become an animal trainer. Moreover, I love the atmosphere at the circus. I'm used to this scene.' These were all the things she said to justify her staying on in this profession. But whatever she said, I just couldn't reconcile to her strange occupation.

Our completely different careers, responsibilities, and indeed, personalities, put a strain on our marriage. Before we married, a friend told us that our marriage would not last long. But at that time, both of us didn't heed his words and instead, turned a deaf ear to all the advice that came our way. She would come up with witticisms that I used to find alluring like 'Our child will be as brave as a tiger and as intelligent as you.'

Let me recapitulate our first meeting. It was the year-end award ceremony at the university. I was drunk after having ingested several glasses of wine. A student proposed that we all go to the circus together to continue the celebrations. This was immediately approved by his companions. The last time I visited the circus was when I was nine years old. Since then, I had not registered any aspect of this entertainment industry.

When we entered the circus, wild applause was just breaking out. Many spectators were standing up to gift flowers to a glowing girl wearing a glittering costume. The overhead beam lights were shining directly into her bright face which had a magnetic smile. Beside her were three huge tigers who were recumbent and docile. I must admit in all honesty that I have never before or since witnessed such a magnificent spectacle.

A petite girl had subdued three fiery, majestic creatures of the jungle. Suddenly, a student pressed a bouquet of violet-red carnations into my hand and pushed me forward, 'Sir, you must go up and give these flowers to a beautiful lady.' At that moment, I was like a zombie. For the first time ever, I found myself on stage giving flowers to an animal trainer! Perhaps it was my silly, earnest face and thick glasses. So out of place in that noisy scenario filled with excited fans, that prompted her to smile at me. 'Perhaps this is the first time that you have come to see us perform, here?' she queried. Up close, I found her even more beautiful with her delicate features and soft, silky hair. What struck me was the freshness of her face that was completely devoid of make-up. Her face was glowing, perhaps lit up from within by the brilliant success of her performance. I realized rather morosely that my career, no matter how successful, would never contain moments of adulation such as hers did. It was perhaps fate that made me utter a sentence that I had never before uttered to any woman before, 'I'm a huge fan of your talent. After the show, if you are free, shall we please meet?' 'Yes, please,' she responded very quietly.

After that, we met several times. We sought each other's company because we came from such different worlds. To quote her, our liaison was an unprecedented coming together of raw strength and intellectualism. We finally decided to get married. It is worth recalling the scene of our wedding. On my side, all the guests were the intellectual elite. These venerable ancients were rather sparing with their smiles or jokes. In contrast, her side was rambunctious. Her guests drank, talked incessantly, laughed loudly and acted in completely crazy ways. At that moment, I realized that I had fallen in love not only with my wife but also with her circus world.

Her circus friends took turns to entertain us. The juggler took four chopsticks and juggled them right there at the wedding party. The magician covered a bowl of soup that had been served with a towel and ordered sternly, 'disappear', and there was no more soup bowl to be seen. Everyone joined in the excited laughter that followed. The clowns were laughing uproariously. Gradually, through the evening, the professors took off their suits and began joining in the fun. Wine flowed like water. A rather inebriated lecturer stood up and serenaded the bride and groom. The song he chose was from 'The Beauty and the Beast'. I was irate. Was this guy implying that I was the beast? Well, I know I'm rather ugly and perhaps not so posh. Then, an acrobat sang in a loud voice: 'At night, let the professor beware of being attacked by tigers.' The horse-trainer joined in shouting, 'The bride should remember to take a whip with her to train her own male-tiger. If he doesn't behave, then she should give him a few lashings with her whip.' Thankfully, my wedding night was not interrupted by tigers nor was I whipped. Though she looked larger than life and completely in command on stage, she was soft and tender in my arms. I hadn't anticipated such gentleness from her. When I mentioned this, she explained, 'The most important quality for an animal trainer to imbibe is the art of loving animals and how to be gentle with them at all times.' Who knows, she has probably taken me to her heart as another beloved animal to be pampered and trained by her!

I must confess, however, that one thing that imprinted itself in my memory after the wedding night was her body odour, and indeed, the stench that emanated from her hair. I later found out that this was the smell of a tiger. What an unforgettable smell!

Well, the honeymoon was soon over and gradually, we settled into a happy married life together. The years passed by. We had very little time together though. She had her winter tours. I too had to travel for my conferences and seminars, both locally and sometimes, overseas. This made every moment we spent together rather precious.

There was nothing about my profession that was of relevance to her. As for her profession, it never ceased to fascinate me. She once told me about her Tô Tô bear who refused to perform. No one understood why. Only later did they find out that it was the day the bears hibernate. Then there was the story of Dak Lak, a massive female tiger more than two metres long and weighing more than one hundred and fifty kilos, who gave birth to her first litter of cubs. A sad but moving story was about a goose, who, during a risk-filled performance, was accidentally trampled on by a horse. As it was dying, it spread its wide wings to embrace its owner. The owner wept bitterly and swore that he would never again train a goose. One day, she showed me a love letter from a fan, which was hidden in the bouquet he had given her.

I wondered if any of her co-performers ever poked fun at her for choosing to marry a University Don! For my part, the teasing was endless. A young, beautiful and unmarried secretary at the university enquired if my wife forced me to jump over a fire-ring. She even brazenly asked me if this female 'tigress' scratched and screamed every time I took her to bed. In the early years, when I went out with my wife, people looked at us with curious eyes . . . as though it was obvious we were a mismatched couple. That really annoyed me and after some time I stopped taking her out anywhere with me.

Only once did I see her looking miserable and confused about her profession. This happened at a friend's birthday party. The owner's dog was friendly with everyone but her. Whenever it came close to her it barked loudly and wanted to bite her. The other ladies there exchanged secret, mocking glances, as if to say 'Look at the tigress fighting'! That was the first time she was so upset and urged me to leave early.

Once we had returned home, she enquired, 'Have you been suffering because I carry the smell of the tiger around with me?' In fact, this was the first time I pinned the pungent smell that she exuded to the tiger. I spoke loving words to comfort her but it was not really a reflection of my true feelings on the subject, 'No, not at all! I love you and love the smell of the tiger'.

She laughed and responded with, 'You are lying. I know you don't like the smell. Last month you made an excuse to not sleep in the same bed declaring that it was rather narrow. All women are expected and permitted to smell good but I am the exception.' I asked her, 'Why not?' and she explained, 'Animals, especially tigers, do not perceive with their eyes as much as sense their surroundings with their noses. A strange smell indicates an enemy,' she continued sadly, 'but this has meant that I have brought the smell of wild beasts into the bedroom and it must have upset you . . .'

The night after she had made up with me, she got into trouble during her performance. When I got there, she was already dead. I was so devastated. I hugged her so tight. With her dark velvet hair, she lay there looking lovely. I could still smell the faint scent of roses that she had exuded the night before. Under the bright lights and in her blood-soaked circus costume, she lay as though she were sleeping. I sobbed. I was heartbroken. I have never felt so desolate in my life. I screamed out in agony, 'Why did you, who surely knew better than anyone about the dos and don'ts of tiger training, still do this? I know ... you did this to please me ... because of my selfishness.' I wanted to jump down the nine levels of hell to be devoured.

The following day, the owner of the circus recounted the events of that fateful day. It seems that the Dak Lak tiger had been ill for a few days previously and had turned violent. It appeared that she had taken exception to her male partner being caged in with another tigress. 'I felt uneasy,' the owner continued. 'I pleaded with her to not go into the animal ring for that one night. But she was intrepid. She confidently said, "No, I'm definitely going in. Animal trainers are not allowed to be afraid or diffident." She then proudly walked on to the stage to a standing ovation.

At first the three tigers demonstrated absolute obedience to her iron control. It was the moment when Dak Lak was to jump over the ring of fire. As the trainer, she stood in front of the tiger and swung her whip through the air to give the alert. The beast jumped up to the high chair. She stepped forward as per routine and raised the ring of fire. It was then that Dak Lak suddenly shrank back. It looked at her with strange eyes. I was on high alert and reached into my holster—hidden under my shirt—for my gun. The tiger was standing there strangely still and poised. She noticed it all standing there. She knew the tiger was about to attack. She also realized that I was going to shoot the beast dead. She shouted out, "Don't shoot". It was at that precise moment that Dak Lak pounced on her like a streak of lightning. It happened in that split second. It was too late. I saw her falling. The stage was in chaos . . . the blood-drunk animal turned around . . . I jumped and fired. My white performing shirt scattered with glitter, now had blood dripping from it. The whole theatre was frozen in horror. As I bent over her, I heard her strained, whispered query. "Is Dak Lak dead? Oh, poor thing. It has four cubs. It wasn't her fault . . . it was mine."

The band, which had also been frozen in terror, suddenly came to life and played a disjointed tune. You know what they say . . . "the show must go on whatever the cost". But no one was in any mood to watch. No one wanted to perform either. Finally, the band too stopped playing. The whole theatre was as quiet as a tomb. Shortly after, she died. I stumbled on to the stage like a blind man choking with misery. The audience refused to leave. The red-eyed clown wandered sightlessly on to the stage unable to take in this deep tragedy.

You must see the number of bouquets and wreaths that have been placed as homage in the spot where she fell.'

Translated from 'Mùi cọp' in
vietmessenger.com

Old Hạc (1943)

Nam Cao (1917–1951)

Old Lão Hạc blew on a stick of dry firewood and lit it. I had already cleared out my long smoking pipe after I had stopped smoking. I then asked him to go first with the pipe but he declined politely.

'Teacher, sir, you should go first'. He passed on the pipe to me and repeated, 'I beg you'.

I then received the pipe, packed in the loose tobacco. After I had taken a deep puff, I passed the pipe back to him. He took in a leisurely puff and finally spoke. He was holding an assortment of things in his hand: a slim firewood stick and an ashtray. He then shared his thoughts with me, 'Maybe I'll sell the dog, Teacher sir'.

He picked up the pipe and smoked again. I inhaled the pungent smoke, creased my eyes like a drunkard and gazed at him pretending to have an interest in his words. In truth I wasn't that bothered by them. I was tired of hearing these same sentiments expressed over and over again. I knew that though he would constantly talk about selling his dog, when it came down to it, he actually never would. Besides, what would it matter if in fact he really did sell it? Why would selling a dog be the cause for such concern?

He took another long puff, put down the pipe and turned aside to exhale the smoke. After a puff of wild tobacco one's brain gets high in a kind of mild ecstasy. Old Hạc sat quietly enjoying that small pleasure. I too sat quietly beside him. My mind wandered back to thinking about my precious books. When I was seriously ill in Saigon, I had sold off most of my clothes. But I couldn't bear to part with even a single one of my books. When I recovered and travelled back to my hometown, my luggage consisted solely of one suitcase packed with books. *Oh, my precious books!* I had vowed to hold on to them for all of my life to preserve the memory of a time past when I was diligent, enthusiastic and ambitious, filled with passion and high hopes. Every time I open a book, even before I start reading, a burning sensation rises in my throat, it is like the breaking of dawn, an image of a crystal clear, hope-filled future that was so much a part of my difficult yet delightful twenties.

Of course, life brings many tribulations. Every time I came to the end of a particular road, I was forced to compromise on my ideals and sell a few of my books to weather the problem. In the end, there were only five books left. But I was resolute that I would keep these with me until my dying day. Yet, last month, I ended up having to see these go too. My little one had dysentery and was completely drained.

'No, old Hạc! I wonder if we have the right to retain something because we want to. I know you love your Vang dog as much as I treasured my books.' But these reflections I kept to myself.

Old Hạc appeared to be pondering over something. He suddenly burst out with, 'It has been a year and my son hasn't sent me even a single letter, Teacher sir.' Ah! So he had been thinking about his son who had been gone for around five or six years to work in a rubber plantation.

When I had first returned to the village, his son's labour contract had expired. Old Hạc had brought me the letter and requested that I read it out to him. It seemed like his son was seeking an extension.

He now briskly explained why his conversation had turned from discussing the dog to talking about his son.

'You see, the dog is his. He bought it. He bought it and raised it, intending to kill it when he married . . .'[38]

That was life! It was always this way. Individuals may plan but may never get to execute their ideas. His son loved a girl. In fact, it was known that both of them were very much in love with each other. The girl's parents acceded to the marriage. But their demands were too much. The bride-price must be a hundred *piastres* and there must be a large quantity of areca fruit and wine. Add to that the wedding cost and the whole cost would have come up to nearly two hundred piastres. Old Hạc couldn't ever afford it. His son wanted him to sell their field to meet the demands. But Hạc didn't allow that. No one sold a family-owned field to get married! Besides, once they sold the field, where would they stay? Moreover, there was no gainsaying what else the bride's family would demand. If they wanted more, even

---

[38] In some parts of Vietnam, people eat dog meat.

selling the field wouldn't be enough. Old Hạc knew all this but he didn't want to command his son to give up the girl. Instead, he tried to explain to him so he would understand the problems. He advised him to give up this girl from a greedy family and after a while to save up for another bride who might be cheaper. 'If you don't marry this girl, you can always marry another. It's not as though the rest of the girls in the village are dead. So, why are you reluctant to give her up?'

Thankfully, the good lad appeared to see his father's point of view. So, he gave up the girl and didn't bring up the topic of his marriage again. But he looked sad. Old Hạc came to know that he was still seeing that girl. It was obvious that he loved her very much. But what can one do? In October that year, the girl got married to the son of the Deputy Headman of the village. The family had property. His son was so furious and desolate. A few days later, he went to the registration centre, presented his identity card and signed the labour contract to work for a rubber plantation . . .

With tears in his eyes, old Hạc recounted:

'Before my son left, he gave me three piastres, Teacher sir. I think he deposited his employment card with his employers and borrowed a few piastres in advance . . . but he gave me three piastres and said, "I'm giving you this cash so that you can have some snacks occasionally. In the past, when I stayed with you, I couldn't make enough money to pay for a single meal. But now that I'm going away, I'm giving you this money so I don't have to worry about you when I'm away. Do collect vegetables from our land and fields and work as a hired labourer. This will bring you enough money for meals. I too will work very hard. I'll come back when I have earned a hundred piastres. Living without money and in dire poverty in this village is not an option because it will only make others look down on us and it is a miserable existence." Now I can only weep for him. I'm helpless to do anything else. Once the employers take the card they keep it forever. It's like he belongs to them from now on. He can never pay them back. He is theirs already. Not my son anymore . . .'

Oh, poor old Hạc! Now I realize why he doesn't want to sell his precious dog. He is all the family that Hạc has left. His wife is dead. His son has gone away. He's old and both day and night are dark and lonely. Who isn't alone? Who doesn't have to combat suffering? When one is sad, having a dog as a companion mitigates unhappiness. Hạc called the dog *cậu Vàng* (boy Vàng) just as a fond, old mother would call her little son. Sometimes, when there was not much else to do, the old man would pick lice off the dog and bathe him at the nearby pond. He would feed it rice in a bowl as though he were a wealthy man. When he had his meal, he shared it with cậu Vàng.

In the evenings, when old Hạc nursed his drink, the dog would dutifully sit at his feet. The old man would feed part of his meal to the dog as though it were a human child. Then, in his love and frustration, he would start cursing it, as though he were parlaying with a child about its father. This is how the conversation would go:

'Do you remember your father, hey, cậu vàng, you? Do you know that your father hasn't sent home a letter for a long time now? He's gone for nearly three years . . . no, more . . . perhaps almost four years . . . I wonder if your father will return later this year! If he does, he will get married and kill you. You had better watch out!'

The dog would look at him all this while, its expression open and guileless. The old man would glare at it, his voice loud and admonitory.

'He plans to kill you, do you understand? If I permit him to do that, you will die, you know.'

The dog would cognize the fact that its master was berating it for some reason and wag its tail fervently in order to appease him. But old Hạc would raise his voice even louder:

'You happy, wagging your tail like that? Well, let me tell you that wagging it so cheerfully is not going to rescue you from your fate. You're gonna die!'

Assuming that the old man was very agitated, the dog would wag its tail even harder and run around him. Then, old Hạc would deftly grab it, hug it, and stroke it gently. He would say, 'Oh no! Never! We'll never kill cậu Vàng. My cậu Vàng is so good. I won't let my son kill you. I will keep cậu Vàng and raise him.' He would then release the dog and pick up his glass to drink his fill. After a while, he would look up, sigh, would mumble something. He would probably have been calibrating the cash he had earned selling the vegetables from his son's field.

After his son's departure, the old man had vowed to preserve the field for his only child. 'This field belongs to my son. When his mother was still alive, she had tightened her belt and was most frugal. She saved up fifty piastres to buy the field. Back then, things had been far cheaper. She had saved up to purchase this property because she was determined that her son should inherit it.' Earlier, when

Hạc's son had wanted to sell the field, he hadn't consented not because he wanted the land for himself but because he wanted to secure his son's future. But back then he hadn't had the money to get married and his son had walked out in frustration. Only when he had earned enough money for his marriage would he return.

Old Hạc was determined that he would save some of the money he made from selling the produce from the garden for his son since the land rightfully belonged to him. Then, when he did return, if he didn't have sufficient funds to get married, Hạc would be in a position to give it to him. If he did have sufficient money, then the extra money would serve as capital for his daughter-in-law and son to pursue some business. He had vowed to do this and he was diligent in pursuing this goal. Hạc worked hard as a hired labourer to make extra money. Whatever money he earned from the yield in the field, he set aside for his son. He was determined that by the time his son returned, he would have saved up a hundred piastres.

But all that had changed. Now, the old man shook his head dejectedly and said:

'Now, all that I saved has disappeared, Teacher sir. I fell ill just once. One bout of illness that lasted exactly two months and eighteen days. During that time I didn't earn a single dong but I had to pay for medicines, and my food. You cannot imagine how much money I lost during that time!'

After the illness, old Hạc became very weak. He was unable to do any heavy work. The village lost the cloth-industry, which had kept so many women employed. As a result, the women of the village had a lot of free time and whenever the call for some light work came up, they all actively competed for it. Therefore, old Hạc found it hard to find employment. Then, the storm arrived. Agricultural crops were destroyed. From that time onwards, Hạc's field did not yield any produce. However, he had to spend three piastres a day on rice for his dog and himself. But this still didn't allay his hunger.

'Actually, cậu Vàng gets better food than I do, Teacher sir,' old Hạc admitted. 'Every day his food alone costs me around a piastre and a half or sometimes two piastres even. This is with a discount. If this continues, where will I find the money to feed the dog? But if I don't feed him well, he will grow thin, and then, we wouldn't get good money when we sell him. Now he's fat and therefore, will bring in a lot of money and people will like to purchase him.'

He paused for a minute and then made an abrupt sound with his tongue.

'Well, that's it! I've decided to sell the dog. Every dong I save in these hard times is worth it. If I spend now, it eats into the money I am saving for my son. Spending to keep the dog healthy will only harm him. Now that I have no means of earning money to compensate for the spending, it would be folly.'

The following day, old Hạc came to visit me. As soon as he set eyes on me, he blurted out, 'cậu Vàng is gone, Teacher sir!'

'Did you sell him?' I enquired.

'Yes. I sold him. They came by to catch him.'

He tried hard to look cheerful. But when I looked at him with a smile, his face filled with tears. I wanted to hug him and cry along. It wasn't because I missed my five books as much as I had earlier but because I felt so sorry for old Hạc.

Just to carry on the painful conversation, I asked, 'So, the dog let these people catch it without any problems?'

His face suddenly convulsed with pain. His wrinkles deepened as slow tears coursed their way down his face. He tilted his head to one side and his toothless mouth twisted as though he were a crying infant. Poor crying, old man!

'Damn it, Teacher sir, it didn't sense a thing. When it saw me calling out, it immediately ran back to me wagging its tail cheerfully. I fed rice to it and it was happily eating when Mục hid himself in the house and came up right behind it and grabbed it by the hind legs and turned my dog upside down. Mục and Xiển struggled briefly before they tied up all four of its legs. Only then did it realize that it was spoken for. What breed of dog is it, Teacher sir, that it's so wise! It looked up at me so sadly as if it couldn't believe my actions . . . as though it blamed me. It grunted as it gazed at me as if to say, "ah, you are so wicked, old master. I gave you my undivided loyalty and love, yet you have treated me so badly." Despite my advanced years, I have cheated a dog who completely trusted me.'

I tried my best to comfort him.

'Hạc, that is just your imagination. In reality, I don't think the dog knew anything. Besides, you are not unique in keeping a dog for a while and then either selling or killing it. If it dies, take comfort from knowing that it is reincarnated to lead another life.'

Old Hạc responded dejectedly, 'No doubt, Teacher sir. One would think that a dog's life is miserable and that if it

reincarnated into a human, perhaps its life would improve…
but not if it is into a human life like mine.'

I cast a glum look at him and replied, 'Everyone's life is
the same. Do you think my life is any better?' That made
Hạc say, 'Well, if human life is also dismal, then what
life form is there that is happy?' He laughed at his own
comment and was racked with cough. I held his thin
shoulders and calmly retorted, 'No, actually life is joyous.
Just being alive is joyful. Now let's both sit down. I'll go
cook some sweet potatoes, boil a pot of thick, fresh tea. We
will both eat the potatoes, drink the tea and smoke a pipe.
That is happiness for us at present.'

'Teacher sir, you are right. For us, right now, this is
happiness.' Saying this, he laughed again. But his laughter,
though gentle, appeared forced.

I said easily, 'All's fine then. Please sit down here. I'll go
and cook the potatoes and boil the water.'

'Oh no! I was only joking, Teacher sir, let's make it
another time,' was Hạc's response.

But I was reluctant to let him go. 'Why should we wait
for another time? The opportunities for being happy occur
rarely and therefore should never be postponed. Please, do
sit down. I'll be quick.'

'Wait! There's one more thing I want to ask.' The old
man's face looked grave.

'What's the matter, old friend?' I enquired gently.

'Let me try to find the words to explain. It's a bit
complicated, Teacher sir.'

'Sure, take your time.'

'Well, it's like this.'

And he spoke at length in a soft voice. It fell roughly under two heads. He began with the fact that he was getting on and his only son was far away. He felt inadequate and inept as he grew older and there was no one to look after him. He thought that it would be difficult for him to work in the field any longer or to continue with his work in the village. He pleaded, 'Teacher sir, you are a learned man, full of knowledge. People respect you. Will you please take care of the three acres of land that rightfully belong to my son?'

He said he would write a letter confirming that I would be the official retainer of the land so that no one would challenge my right to take care of the land and also, no one would dare to occupy the land illegally. He said that when his son returned, even though he could take over the garden, the land document would still be under my name so that I would be able to ensure its security.

The next thing he said was that he was old and frail and wasn't sure how long he would live nor when he would die. With his only child being far away, he was troubled at the thought that if he died there would be no one to take care of his funeral. He wouldn't die in peace, he said, if he thought that his funeral expenses would have to be borne by his neighbours. So, he carefully took out his savings, painfully earned over a long period through hard labour: thirty piastres in total, of which twenty-five were from his savings and five piastres were from selling the dog. He was insistent that I take the money and in case he died, to reassure the neighbours that the bulk of the funeral expenses would already be paid for and they would just have to contribute a little towards it.

I tried to cheer him up and attempted to joke, 'Why do you worry so much? You are still very healthy. You have a long way to go before you die. Why do you have such morbid thoughts? Go out and enjoy your hard-earned money. Eat well now. What's the point in worrying about what would happen after your death? Why save now at the risk of starving yourself?'

'Teacher sir, if I enjoy good food now with that money, how will you take care of my funeral expenses? I know you mean well and your advice is sensible. But no matter how much I earn from working my son's field, I find that I'm not able to save much. My son is single. He has no wife or children. If he cannot find other means to survive, he will at least have the land to fall back on. I am bowing and pleading with you. I'm prepared to do anything to persuade you. Please understand my situation and help an old man by keeping this money carefully for me.'

When I saw how distressed he looked, I yielded and accepted the money. As he was leaving, I asked him anxiously, 'But if you give me all your savings, old Hạc, how are you going to survive?'

He smiled rather sadly. 'Don't worry! I've already planned for it . . . all things must come to an end.'

From then on, every few days, when I checked on old Hạc, I found him resorting to eating an odd assortment of things. For a few days, he only ate potatoes. Once these were gone, his meals became even more erratic. One day he would eat a banana tuber and the next, boiled figs. I even found him eating *Gotu kola* (spade leaf) and sometimes just a few tubers or ốc (a meal of mussels or shellfish). I was concerned about his wretched state and raised the topic with my wife. But she brushed it off.

'Well, let the old man die. He has money. No one asked him to suffer. He has brought this upon himself. We are not any better off than him. So, how can we help him? Even our child goes hungry many times . . ' she would retort.

Alas! Human nature is such that it leads people to label others as crazy, stupid, mean, disgusting, or ugly rather than try to understand them. We find many excuses to be cruel to others. We never sympathize with them nor see them as people who deserve our pity. My wife is not a bad person but she is always unhappy. Can a person with an injured foot ever overcome his pain to think of his neighbour's needs? When one is drowning in one's own sorrow and suffering, it is difficult to care for others. Their natural generosity gets occluded by their own fears, worries, and sorrows. I understand this but it still makes me . . . not upset . . . more angry and sad.

I tried to help old Hạc secretly, hiding this from my wife. But he seemed to sense my wife's antipathy and so refused all help. Sometimes he would do so stridently. And, gradually, he started drifting away from me.

It made me sadder still to realize that old Hạc didn't understand my motivations. Often, poor people who have a lot of pride become prickly when you offer to help them. They are sensitive and don't want to be objects of pity. It is indeed hard to help them. I complained about this to Binh Tư, another neighbour, one day. He was a bit of a rogue and so didn't like honest old Hạc very much. He scowled and remarked, 'Oh, he's just pretending. He just looks deep and contemplative. In actual fact, he is very calculating and not as innocent and sensitive as everyone thinks he is. He just asked me for some dog bait . . .'

I opened my eyes wide in surprise. He continued in a slightly hushed voice, 'Hạc said there was a dog that keeps wandering into his field and he plans to poison it. If he succeeds, he and I plan to get together to drink rice wine and eat dog meat.'

I was shocked.

Old Hạc, I thought to myself, *so even you are not as transparently good as I had supposed. You are no better than the average man. How could I have been so fooled by you! A man who had once cried to me for having tricked his dog . . . a man who starved to save for his funeral because he didn't want to be beholden to his neighbours nor trouble them in any way.* And such a man now plots with Binh Tư to trap a dog for his meal! *How disillusioning*, I thought.

Well, life can be deceptive but not in ways we anticipate. When I returned home from meeting Binh Tu, I heard a commotion in old Hạc's house. I hurried over to investigate. Quite a few neighbours were buzzing around and I rushed in to find out what was going on.

Old Hạc lay writhing in his bed. His hair was disheveled and his clothes were in disarray. His eyes were rolling wildly. He was screaming with pain and foaming at the mouth. His whole body jerked periodically and he seemed to leap off the bed so much so that two strong men were holding him down to prevent that. He struggled thus for two long hours before finally dying. His death was truly brutal.

No one could make sense of this sudden and painful illness that had assailed old Hạc. Only Binh Tư and I knew the truth behind his strange convulsions and terrible death. But we didn't see any point in enlightening people about the real cause.

Dear old Hạc, please go in peace. Don't worry about your field. I will look after it. When your son returns, I will give it back to him and I will tell him, 'This is the land that your father, who raised you, tried to leave intact for you. He was prepared to die rather than sell even a minuscule portion of it . . .'

Translated from Nam Cao. *Nam Cao-Tác phẩm*, tập 1 (NXB Văn học, Hà Nội, 1975)